HOOPS

HOOPS

The Complete Guide

to Basketball

and the NBA

by Godfrey Jordan

RANDOM HOUSE OF CANADA

For Thomas, Patrick and Anne

Canadian Cataloguing in Publication Data

Jordan, G. P. (Godfrey P.)
   Hoops: the complete guide to basketball and the NBA

ISBN 0-394-22454-X

1. Basketball - Juvenile literature.
2. National Basketball Association - Juvenile literature.
I. Title.

GV885.1.J67 1995   j796.323   C95-931256-0

Please see page 155 for a full list of illustration and photo credits.

Cover photograph: © Nathaniel S. Butler/NBA Photos
Cover and interior design: Sharon Foster Design

Printed and bound in Canada

10 9 8 7 6 5 4 3 2 1

CONTENTS

Coming Home: Basketball's Roots in Canada 7

Introduction 9

CHapTEr 1
Let's Invent a New Game! 11

ChapTer 2
Basket + Ball + Other Stuff, Too 15

CHapter 3
Playing by the Rules: Then and Now 23

Chapter 4
B-Ball Basics 33

ChapTEr 5
Take Your Positions 47

CHAPter 6
Helping It All Happen:
Officials, Coaches, Trainers 54

ChaptER 7
The NBA: Yesterday and Today 73

ChApter 8
The Year That Is a Season 79

ChAPTEr 9
Hoop History Highlights 90

CHapTer 10
Love Those Numbers! 107

ChapteR 11
The Basketball Hall of Fame 120

ChapTER 12
The Court Speaks 124

CHaPteR 13
NBA Team Directory 137

CHApTer 14
Superstar Statistics 147

Acknowledgements 153

Photograph and Illustration Credits 155

Coming Home:
Basketball's Roots in Canada

Hoops comes home! The excitement raised by the Toronto Raptors and Vancouver Grizzlies joining the National Basketball Association brings the game full circle in Canadian sports history.

Consider:

- The fact that Dr. James Naismith of Almonte, Ontario, invented basketball has been well documented. However, that Naismith organized the first game *outside* Canada doesn't diminish our country's contribution to the sport. At least 10 of the players in that first game were university students from Quebec.

- Basketball played by school and local amateur teams has been part of the Canadian scene since the turn of the century.

- The Grads, a women's team from Edmonton, competed in the Olympics until 1936 and won 27 games in a row. Unfortunately medals were not awarded at that time for women's competition. Career win/loss record: 502–20.

- Canada played the final match in the 1936 Olympics, the first time basketball was recognized as a medal sport. Our national team lost the gold to the United States, playing outdoors in the rain-soaked championship final in Berlin. The score, 19–8.

- The NBA's very first game was played at Maple Leaf Gardens, on November 1, 1946, with the New York Knicks against the Toronto Huskies.

- Montreal hosted the 1976 Olympics, at which women's basketball finally entered official medal competition.

- In 1994, the World Championship of Basketball came to North America for the first time, with the top 16 international teams playing off against each other in Toronto and Hamilton.

Now, with the Raptors and Grizzlies taking to the court, Canadians can share in the special kind of excitement that pro basketball delivers.

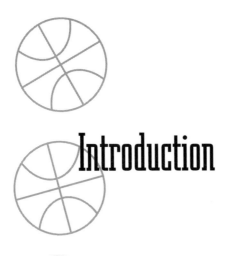

Introduction

It began when a young Canadian was asked to come up with an indoor activity for wintertime play. James Naismith decided to attach a pair of peach baskets to the balcony of a YMCA gymnasium. He never planned to launch a sport that would captivate the world. Since that afternoon back in 1891, the game has continued to grow so rapidly that it is now played wherever a hoop can hang and a ball can be thrown into it.

Basketball allows an athlete every opportunity to demonstrate superb abilities. It's more than just shooting at a net: the sport gives you a chance to prove excellence in teamwork as well as individual skill. The speed and intensity displayed at the professional level make it one of the most satisfying spectator sports.

Action. Amazing feats.

A chance to put gravity on hold.

Basketball gives you all that, plus much more. And to see it played at the absolute best, look to the National Basketball Association.

As their stars proved beyond doubt in the Barcelona Olympics and the World Championship of Basketball, only one league can fill a lineup that deserves the title "Dream Team."

HOOPS gives you a "fast break" inside the action: what sparks the NBA, where it's been, how it's played, why things happen and what to look for next.

It's not only *The Complete Guide to Basketball and the NBA*, it's another reason to say, "I love this game!"

Let's Invent a New Game!

First, The Dream

When Shaquille O'Neal was a youngster, he would take a ball onto a court and play a game by himself called "Dreamful Attraction."

"I'd go out there alone and shoot, thinking 'Shaq versus Dr. J' and do the moves going around him to score. I spent a lot of time by myself playing that," says the NBA superstar. "And it paid off."

That solitary game imagined by the Orlando Magic center has its roots in a quest dreamed up just over a century ago. Unlike other sports, whose origins may be clouded in myth and rumor, basketball can pinpoint its birth to an exact time and place.

December 1891. Springfield, Massachusetts.

At the Young Men's Christian Association Training School, Luther Gulick had a problem on his hands. Too many of the students complained of the boring athletics available during the cold New England winter. After months outdoors playing baseball, soccer, rugby and football, the main activity was gymnastics. Many found it too limiting. The dean of physical education asked one of his staff to come up with an alternative.

However, Dean Gulick placed a few restrictions on this assignment. Since the game was to be played indoors, he did not want it to cause injury through physical contact. A number of men should be able to play it all at the same time, giving them lots of exercise. Finally, it should be easy to learn, but require a level of skill in order to hold the students' interest.

An early basketball, durable but difficult to bounce.

James Naismith got the chore. He was an enthusiastic athlete who loved playing rugby, football and lacrosse. Born and raised in Almonte, Ontario, the young man had left his Canadian home to devote himself to studies at the International YMCA School. Naismith's dream was to combine a love of sports with the pursuit of higher ideals.

Naismith thought about the popularity of outdoor sports. They were games often making use of a ball passed among team players, who then scored by placing it in a goal their opponents tried to defend.

Naismith went into the school's gymnasium and looked around. On the floor he saw a rugby ball and a soccer ball; he picked up the soccer ball. His eyes rose to the balcony surrounding the gym, 10 feet above the floor. With a burst of inspiration, he imagined a game in which you tossed a ball into a goal positioned over the heads of your opponents.

His Canadian background playing lacrosse and hockey may have helped him think about the need for special skills. So did "Duck on a Rock," a game Naismith knew from Ontario lumber camps. The object of the game was to use one rock to knock another rock off a ledge. He remembered how the winners did not "throw" their rock, but "tossed" it in an arc. This kind of shot seemed to be more successful in dislodging the target. A skillful shot was necessary, rather than a powerful one.

With all that in mind, and adhering to Dean Gulick's requirements, James Naismith wrote down 13 rules. Not in his wildest dreams could the good doctor from Almonte, Ontario, have imagined that he had just invented one of the world's most versatile, popular sports.

Then The Reality

It became time to put theory into practice. But the game nearly became "boxball."

That's because Naismith asked the school custodian, "Pop" Stebbins, to bring him two boxes, about 18 inches square.

Maybe the janitor found something silly about this whole idea, or he just didn't bother emptying the trash containers used in the school's kitchen. Instead he picked up a pair of empty peach baskets.

James Naismith took the two baskets from Stebbins. They were "to be fastened at each end of the gymnasium to the balcony," which just happened to be 10 feet above the floor. The height of the basket remains exactly that today.

Next he recruited the 18 students of his class and named two captains. Each captain chose a team of nine players. Naismith explained the 13 rules to these "first round-ever!-draft picks" and then tossed the ball up at center court for the sport's first tip-off.

When the team asked what the game might be called, one player suggested "Naismith ball." James Naismith waved off the proposal. Frank Mahan, a team captain, then stated, "Why not call it Basket Ball?" And so it was.

From that moment on, this new game caught the fascination of players and spectators. The Springfield gymnasium began to attract visitors who had heard of this wonderful game that chased winter away.

The graduates of Springfield's Training College went across North America — and around the world — to work and teach at other YMCAs. They brought not only their educational skills, but also a bubbling enthusiasm for this new sport.

Basket + Ball + Other Stuff, Too

2

Before an NBA superstar ever steps onto the hardwood floor of a crowded arena, he has spent many hours getting familiar with the tools of his trade: a ball and a hoop. This simplicity of the game is its universal appeal.

The Ball

The first basketballs were not very reliable. Leather sections were laced together over an inflatable rubber bladder. They differed in size and "bounceability," but at least they were round.

When Spalding Sporting Goods published the "Official Basket Ball Rules" in 1896, the company declared their own product, an 18- to 20-ounce ball, as the standardized official ball. Stronger leather was used over the years to improve the ball's durability.

The process for manufacturing basketballs leaped ahead in 1935 when Milton Reach of Spalding patented a molded ball built around a thin hollow sphere, or "last" of wax. This Last-Bilt ball became the official ball in 1950.

Tan-and-black leather was the choice of most coaches and players for basketballs in the early days. But even white balls were an option. Until 1957, the home team could choose the color for that day's game: tan or yellow.

Then the eye of television began to focus more clearly on basketball. An orange ball proved to be the most telegenic, and in 1960 it became the standard game ball.

Spalding, which produced the first basketball in 1894, is today the official supplier for the National Basketball Association. At the beginning of every season, each NBA team receives a supply of 50 official NBA game balls.

That's just a tiny fraction of the 40 million Spalding basketballs sold each year. Although they are manufactured primarily in Korea, each ball used in the NBA is first sent to the Spalding factory in Chicopee, Massachusetts, for special testing.

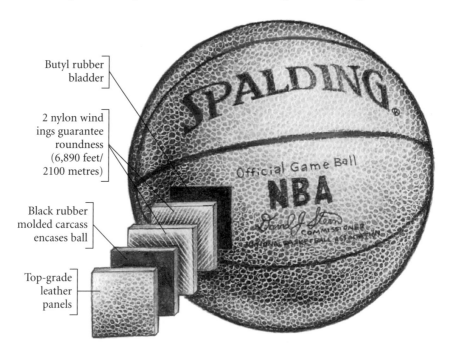

Butyl rubber bladder

2 nylon windings guarantee roundness (6,890 feet/ 2100 metres)

Black rubber molded carcass encases ball

Top-grade leather panels

... how a basketball is made?

A Spalding official NBA game ball begins with the selection of top-grain cowhide. The hide is cured in a process using extracts from the bark of trees, a tanning method that goes back to prehistoric times.

The inner part of the ball is constructed from a molded bladder around which is wound 6,890 feet (2100 m) of adhesive-coated nylon thread. The rubber carcass is then heat-moulded over the wound bladder.

In the tannery, the leather hides are inserted into a giant press that imbeds tiny pebbles into the grain. These "pebbles" give the ball its distinctive texture and the firm grip that a player needs.

The leather panels are handcrafted and cemented onto the sealed carcass, then returned to a cold mold, where 140 pounds of pressure are inserted in the ball. This forces out any tiny air bubbles, so the inside portion will stick thoroughly against the outside panels. In its final state, the ball measures between 29 1/2 and 29 7/8 inches in circumference, and is inflated to an air pressure of between 7 1/2 and 8 1/2 pounds per square inch.

That's how you end up with *bamada-bamada-bamada* — the sweet sound of a bouncing basketball.

Constant inspection throughout its manufacture guarantees that every official NBA game ball gives a player a perfect ball!

Three official game balls must be provided for each NBA game by the home team.

At least six balls are to be available to each team for the pregame warm-ups.

Unlike other sports such as hockey or baseball, a spectator doesn't get a take-home souvenir if the basketball bounces into the stands.

You're left only with that memory of letting the game continue because you returned the ball to the sidelines, where it was thrown back in play!

The Basket

As the game became more popular, those first peach baskets took a battering. A stronger target was needed. By 1895, rules called for an 18-inch metal rim to be suspended 10 feet above the floor, with hammock nets of cord 18 inches deep hanging from the rim.

A score counted only when the ball went through the ring and remained in the net. The referee then climbed a ladder to remove the ball or poked it loose with a stick. What a way to cool down a hot scoring team! It wasn't until 1912 that a rule called for the bottom of the net to be opened. Finally a ball was permitted to fall through and count as a score.

Even though other types of baskets (chainlinked, leather, cloth or rubber-rimmed) and different heights have been toyed with, the 10-foot-high netted ring has remained the standard.

Today the basket consists of a pressure-release metal safety ring 18 inches in inside diameter, with a white cord net hanging 15 to 18 inches in length. The ring is painted orange and is just six inches from the backboard at its closest point. The cord net is attached by a dozen loops, designed to check the ball momentarily, slowing it down as it passes through the basket.

The Backboard

The first backboard was created in 1893 to prevent "fan interference." Spectators would sit in the balcony just above where the basket hung. Depending on which team was shooting, they would lean over either to block the shot or guide the ball into the basket.

By 1895, wire backboards were used. Often they worked to the advantage of the home team. Players would slightly bend or indent the wire so that the ball could more easily slide into the top of the basket. Wood backboards became the rule in 1904.

The transparent backboard came into use in 1946 to give spectators a better view of the action. The following year, a rectangle was painted above the basket to provide the players with a target for better aiming.

With an increase in jumping ability and more play "above the rim," special padding was added in 1966 to the bottom and lower sides of the backboard for the players' protection.

The Uniform

Every NBA team has two sets of jerseys. A light-colored uniform is always worn by the home team; the visitors dress in dark colors. Their shorts and socks match their jerseys.

A player's number appears on the front and back of his jersey. The numbers are 3/4 inch wide and six inches high.

The player's surname is on the back of his sweater, in letters two inches high. If another player on the team has the same last name, each adds his first initial, as well.

Jewelry of any sort is not permitted to be worn by any player during a game. Those who require braces, splints, casts or face protectors must use padded or foam-covered material that does not have any sharp or cutting edges. Approval for wearing these must come from the officials before every game.

The basketball shoes worn by players are built to withstand rugged action. Since the game revolves around stop-and-run moves with quick turns and quick leaps, proper foot support and ankle protection are vital. High tops are favored by most, because they cover the ankle. Shoes also need to cushion the impact of every move and leap. A hard sole with some bounce provides the best shock absorption.

The Court

The playing court for all National Basketball Association games is 94 feet long by 50 feet wide. A two-inch-wide line marks all the boundaries.

The flooring for most NBA home courts is comprised of four-by-eight-foot panels of maple about 3/4 of an inch thick. Its surface is treated with a clear polyurethane. The panels are fitted onto an aluminum track frame to keep everything in place.

A scorer's table is set at midcourt, at least three feet back from the outer boundary of the court. The seats of any team or spectators must also be the same distance back.

The game begins in the jump-ball circle at the center of the court.

Two baskets are placed at opposite ends of the court. The foul lanes marked by "the paint" in front of each basket extend to another jump ball circle, making this resemble a "key."

But in Boston...

The famous parquet that the Celtics have played on since day one (i.e., 1946) has been rebuilt and added to over the years. Some original pieces of the one-inch solid-oak flooring are said to remain in it today.

Before the demolition of the Boston Garden, the hallowed oak was transported in the summer of 1995 to the Celtics' new premises. Tongue-and-groove connectors hold the five-by-five-foot panels securely in place after assembly. That gives the new FleetCenter not only the historic parquet but also a foundation on which to revive the Celtics' tradition!

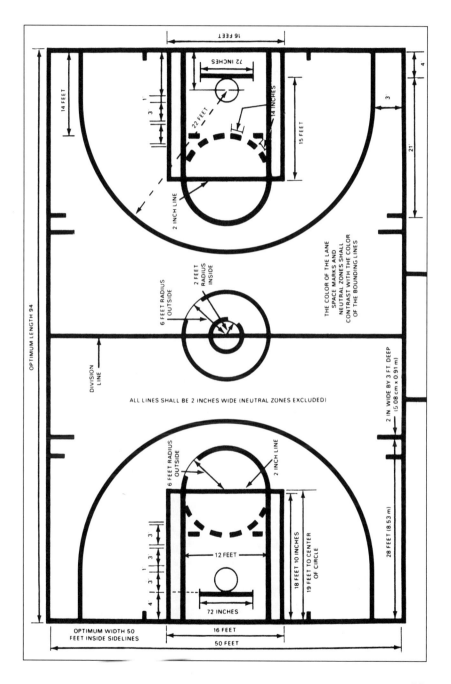

OPTIMUM LENGTH 94

16 FEET

72 INCHES

14 FEET

72 INCHES

22 FEET

14 INCHES

2 INCH LINE

15 FEET

4

3

21'

THE COLOR OF THE LANE
SPACE MARKS AND
NEUTRAL ZONES SHALL
CONTRAST WITH THE COLOR
OF THE BOUNDING LINES

2 FEET
RADIUS
INSIDE

6 FEET RADIUS
OUTSIDE

DIVISION
LINE

ALL LINES SHALL BE 2 INCHES WIDE (NEUTRAL ZONES EXCLUDED)

2 IN. WIDE BY 3 FT. DEEP
(5.08 cm x 0.91 m)

6 FEET RADIUS
OUTSIDE

2 INCH LINE

12 FEET

18 FEET 10 INCHES

19 FEET TO CENTER
OF CIRCLE

28 FEET (8.53 m)

3

1

3

1

3

4

72 INCHES

OPTIMUM WIDTH 50
FEET INSIDE SIDELINES

16 FEET

50 FEET

21

. . . .

. . . on the top floor of the Supreme Court Building in Washington, D.C., there is a gymnasium with a basketball court? It is used by federal employees during lunch breaks and after-hours for relaxation. Because of its location atop the offices of the Supreme Court Building, it's known as the highest "court" in the land.

. . . .

Dr. James Naismith gives some basketball tips to his wife
Maude (Sherman) Naismith.

PLAYING BY THE RULES: THEN AND NOW

Then...

James Naismith's Original 13 Rules (December 1891)

The object of the game is to put the ball into your opponents' goal. This may be done by throwing the ball from any part of the grounds, with one or both hands, under the following conditions and rules:

The ball to be an ordinary Association foot ball.

1. *The ball may be thrown in any direction with one or both hands.*

2. *The ball may be batted in any direction with one or both hands (never with a fist).*

3. *A player cannot run with the ball. The player must throw it from the spot on which he catches it, allowance to be made for a man who catches the ball when running if he tries to stop.*

4. *The ball must be held by the hands. The arms or body must not be used for holding it.*

5. No shouldering, holding, pushing, tripping, or striking in any way the person of an opponent shall be allowed; the first infringement of this rule by any player shall count as a foul, the second shall disqualify him until the next goal is made, or, if there was evident intent to injure the person, for the whole of the game, no substitute allowed.

6. A foul is striking at the ball with the fist, violation of Rules 3, 4 and such as described in Rule 5.

7. If either side makes three consecutive fouls it shall count as a goal for the opponents (consecutive means without the opponents in the meantime making a foul).

8. A goal shall be made when the ball is thrown or batted from the grounds into the basket and stays there, providing those defending the goal do not touch or disturb the goal. If the ball rests on the edges, and the opponent moves the basket, it shall count as a goal.

9. When the ball goes out of bounds, it shall be thrown into the field of play by the person first touching it. He has a right to hold it unmolested for five seconds. In case of a dispute the umpire shall throw it straight into the field. The thrower-in is allowed five seconds; if he holds it longer it shall go to the opponent. If any side persists in delaying the game the umpire shall call a foul on that side.

10. The umpire shall be the judge of the men and shall note the fouls and notify the referee when three consecutive fouls have been made. He shall have power to disqualify men according to Rule 5.

11. The referee shall be judge of the ball and shall decide when the ball is in play, in bounds, to which side it belongs, and shall keep the time. He shall decide when a goal has been made and keep account of the goals, with any other duties that are usually performed by a referee.

12. The time shall be two fifteen minute halves, with five minutes' rest between.

13. The side making the most goals in that time shall be declared the winner. In the case of a draw the game may, by agreement of the captains, be continued until another goal is made.

And Now...

The regulations first posted on a wall just over a century ago have become the cornerstone for the National Basketball Association's set of 12 rules. These have since evolved to take into account nearly every imaginable situation, detailed in 93 sections with over 500 subsections and articles. Additional comments on those rules also apply.

And just in case a completely unanticipated incident arises during the game, the officials do have the power (Rule 2, Section III) to make decisions on any point not specifically covered in the rules.

For the fan sitting courtside or watching the action on television, the essential points are:

Game Length

- All NBA games are made up of two halves (each 24 minutes in length) with a 15-minute rest between halves.

- Each half has two periods, or quarters, of 12 minutes each, with a two-minute break between them.

- Overtime periods, to decide a tie game, are five minutes long.

Play Begins

- At the opening tip-off in the center jump ball circle, the referee tosses the ball up and it reaches maximum height before being touched.

- Starting the second and third quarters, the team that lost the opening tap puts the ball into play from the opponents' end line.

- For the fourth period, the team that gained possession at the opening tap throws the ball in from their opponents' end line.

- An overtime period starts with a center jump ball.

Scoring Points

- A score occurs when a ball successfully falls through the basket from above.

- One point is scored on each free throw (if the shot is successful) by a player who has been fouled and awarded a free throw on the penalty.

- Two points are scored on a field goal, a successful shot that isn't a free throw taken from on or inside the three-point line.

- Three points are awarded on a basket scored from beyond the three-point line, a semi-circle marked 22 feet away from the net.

The 24-Second Clock

- Whenever a team gains possession of the ball, a clock begins counting down from the 24-second mark.

- If a shot does not hit the rim or the backboard before the 24-second time limit runs out, the team must hand over possession of the ball to the opponents.

The Ball is Dead

- If it gets stuck around the basket and the backboard or hits the back of the backboard or its supports.

- At a free throw that is the first of multiple attempts.

- When it goes over the outside boundary lines, unless a player who might be airborne and has not stepped out of bounds knocks it back in play.

- When an official's whistle blows.

- At a personal foul, fighting foul or floor violation.

- Before the throw-in that follows a field goal or successful free throw.

- When time expires at the end of a period (unless the ball is in flight).

A Regular Timeout

- Lasts 100 seconds (one minute and 40 seconds).

- Must be called twice in every period.

- Can be requested by a player only when the ball is dead or his own team has possession of it.

- Each team is permitted seven regular timeouts.

- If no timeout has been called with 6:59 left in a quarter, the official scorer calls a timeout at the next dead ball and assesses it to the home team.

- If neither team has taken another timeout with 2:59 remaining in a quarter, the official scorer imposes a timeout at the next dead ball against the team not previously charged.

- No more than four timeouts can be taken by a team in the fourth quarter, with a maximum of three timeouts in the game's final two minutes.

- Extra timeouts result in a technical foul, with the opposing team granted a free throw.

- In overtime, a team is allowed three timeouts and may take them at any time during each overtime period.

A 20-Second Timeout

- Each team is allowed one 20-second timeout per half; overtime is considered an extension of the second half.

- Can be requested by a player only when the ball is dead or his own team has possession of it.

- The player must specify "20-second timeout" or the official determines it as a regular timeout.

- Any extra 20-second timeout requests are charged as full, regular timeouts.

Substitutions

- A player may enter the game by notifying the scorer who he is to replace and then waiting in the substitution box in front of the scorer's table.

- As soon as the ball is dead, the scorer sounds a horn to indicate a substitution.

- The player waits for an official to signal him onto the court; if not, he is charged with a technical foul.

- No substitute can take a free throw resulting from a technical foul.

- Unless selected by the opposing coach to replace an injured teammate, a substitute shall not take a jump ball or replace a free-throw shooter.

- Each team can make only one substitution during a 20-second timeout, with the defensive team doing so only if the other team does so (more than one substitution per team in this case requires a full timeout to be called).

- A player can be replaced and reenter the game as a substitute during the same dead ball.

A Personal Foul

- Refers to physical interference with an opponent.

- Also known as a "common foul."

- Examples: tripping, charging, elbowing, pushing, holding and blocking; dribbling into an opponent or through an area where there isn't enough space to go without making contact; forcing a dribbler to run into another defensive player by screening or crowding a player.

- Penalty: free throw for defensive fouls; for offensive fouls (excluding punching, elbow or flagrant foul) loss of possession.

- Upon his sixth personal foul, a player is disqualified and "fouls out" of the game.

A Technical Foul

- Can be committed by a player, team, coach or assistants.

- Examples: unnecessary game delay; harassing an official or unsportsmanlike actions; taking more than seven timeouts during the game; illegal defenses that violate league guidelines prohibiting certain tactical arrangements on the court.

- A free throw is awarded for most technical fouls: the shooter stands alone, with no one positioned along the free-throw lane.

A Violation

- Is an infraction against the rules of basketball.

- The ball becomes dead (eliminating any point that may have scored when the violation was called).

- Typical violations include: running with the ball; kicking the ball intentionally; striking the ball with the fist; controlling the ball in your backcourt for more than 10 seconds without bringing it across the center line; taking more than five seconds for a throw-in; offensive players remaining in the free throw lane for more than three seconds; bringing the ball into your own backcourt.

- Penalty is loss of possession, with a throw-in by the opponents.

A Free Throw

- Also known as "foul shot," since it is awarded to a player who has been fouled.

- The ball is handed by an official to the player, who stands behind the free-throw line in the circle at the top of the foul lane.

- The shooter has just 10 seconds to take a free throw.

- If the opponents hinder or interfere, another free throw is added.

- A bonus free throw is awarded upon a team's fifth personal foul in a quarter.

- After a free throw, the player remains behind the line until the ball strikes the rim or backboard.

- If the player is successful and a second free throw has not been awarded, play resumes with a throw-in by the opponents from their end line.

- The ball is in play if the free throw did not score, and is not followed by another attempt.

The Game is Over

- At the end of the second half if one team has scored more points than its opponent.

- If there is a tie game, the teams continue to play five-minute overtime periods until there is a winner at the end of any extra period.

A Reminder...

The preceding points are meant to provide an overview of the rules. For the complete, unabridged version, you'll have to consult "The Official Rules of the NBA," detailed in the following categories:

Rule 1 - Court Dimensions and Equipment

Rule 2 - Officials and Their Duties

Rule 3 - Players, Substitutes and Coaches

Rule 4 - Definitions

Rule 5 - Scoring and Timing

Rule 6 - Putting Ball in Play; Live/Dead Ball

Rule 7 - 24-Second Clock

Rule 8 - Out-of-Bounds and Throw-in

Rule 9 - Free Throw

Rule 10 - Violations and Penalties

Rule 11 - Basketball Interference — Goaltending

Rule 12 - Fouls and Penalties

B-Ball Basics 4

Played well, basketball is a series of continuous actions occurring everywhere on the court. Each game moves to a particular rhythm and beat. Players require tremendous physical stamina as they try to position themselves for an open shot, a better pass, a higher rebound, or as they shift defensively to stop those plays from being completed.

The National Basketball Association may have the fittest athletes in professional sports. With the number of fast breaks, sudden stops, pivots, jumps and turns that make up every game, there is no place in the lineup for anyone in less than peak physical condition.

To maintain themselves in top shape, players usually follow an individual fitness program. Jogging, cycling, aerobics and weight training are part of the program, but before a game muscles still need a careful tune-up.

Warming Up to The Game

Pregame exercises are an essential part of an NBA player's routine. Many fans never get a chance to see this exercise ritual.

The sight of their heroes lying on the floor to loosen up is not the image that comes to mind for warm-ups. But these exercises are just as important as the shooting drills that take place a short while afterward.

Pregame exercises lessen a player's chance of injury. The athletes carefully stretch muscles that take the brunt of the game's activities.

Leg exercises are most important, since they help to withstand the game's running, stopping and pounding jumps. Players will work on stretching their calf, hamstring and groin muscles to prevent tears or spasms that could pull them from a game. Knees and ankles, once loosened up, may require some padding or taping for added safety.

Next comes the upper body. The arms, shoulders and back need to become loose and relaxed and free of the tension created by tight muscles. A variety of slow and steady exercises not only awaken these muscles but alert the mind to prepare for strenuous play.

With a team's fortune riding on the good health of its players, none can afford to take shortcuts when it comes to warm-ups.

The Stance

While TV highlights favor the shots on basket, it's the ball control and handling before the goal that makes everything happen. The dribble or pass to start the play is founded on steady footwork; it all begins with the stance.

For a player without the ball, his knees should be bent slightly and he should be balanced on the balls of the feet, which are shoulder-width apart. One foot, the pivot, is placed slightly behind the other. The player's back is upright and his head remains steady, as he looks straight on at the action. His elbows are close to the body, with the palms of the hand facing outward, ready to take a pass, make a steal or block a shot. This all-purpose stance allows a player to shift quickly to either side, to advance or retreat.

If holding the ball, the player assumes the same position as the player without the ball, but he uses his hip to shield the ball. This stance gives him the option of getting off a set shot or jumper, moving to make a pass or driving in for a layup.

Basketball's footwork is based on the pivot. That's the foot a player uses to turn around on after getting a pass or in preparing to make a play. Right-handed players tend to favor the left foot as their pivot. The pros use both equally well.

If a player changes his pivot foot — or lifts it — while still holding the ball, a violation known as "walking" is called. The penalty is loss of possession.

The Dribble

Good ball handling begins with the dribble. It's such a basic skill in the game that it's often overlooked — and sometimes overused.

Dribbling is about movement and control. It may be necessary for moving the ball down the court. But passing is much faster. Dribbling keeps the ball under control until you can pass to a teammate or take a shot yourself. Meanwhile your opponents can set up a defense.

The dribble is really a controlled bounce, using the fingertips to move the ball downward with a flicking motion. The bounce should rise back up to the space between the knees and the waist.

As the player dribbles with either hand, sometimes crossing over or changing from one hand to the other, the ball has to be protected from the opponent. That means keeping your body between the ball and the other person. Holding the other arm up, chest-high, lets the player fend off an opponent.

The dribbler has to keep his head up, as he constantly looks around the court — not at the ball — because at some point the dribbling will stop and a play must be made.

If the area is crowded, the player will use a low dribble: he'll keep the ball bouncing below knee-level to maintain protective control.

With no obstructions and no one open for a pass, the high — or speed — dribble comes into play. It sometimes happens as a result of a steal. The ball is pushed ahead, at such an angle that the player running downcourt is able to meet up with it at the next bounce. He can move it forward again or grab it and try a shot.

Dribbling Don'ts:

Using one hand to steady the ball while dribbling.

Using both hands at the same time to dribble.

Moving without dribbling (that's "traveling," "steps," or "walking").

• • •

The penalty for all of the above is loss of possession.

Effective dribbling is a way to avoid giving up the ball to an opponent. Here are two examples:

A behind-the-back dribble has a player using his body to block the ball as he moves it out of view from one hand to the other.

The crossover dribble has the ball pushed across and down, then back up in the other hand, as the player races past the opponent.

The Pass

Teamwork sparkles in the passing plays. The objective is to move the ball among teammates until it ends up with the player who is in the best position to shoot.

A superior ability to "feed the ball" to an open teammate keeps the opponents guessing what sort of play will develop next. It puts them on the defensive and lessens their own attack.

Five common types of passes are used in every game.

The *chest pass* snaps from the thrower's chest, elbows in at the side, as the player steps toward the receiver, who should get the ball at his own chest-level. The floor should be open between these players to prevent an opponent from knocking the ball down with his arms.

In cases where there might be a defender between the passer and intended receiver, the *bounce pass* is employed. Using the same movement as the chest pass, the thrower targets an area on the floor that is two-thirds on the way to his receiver. The ball smacks downward, under and past any defenders, then angles back up to his teammate.

The *overhead pass* might begin as a faked chest pass, used to confuse a defender. The difference comes when the arms are quickly raised above the head, elbows in, and the pass is delivered with a snap of the wrists as the arms are extended. It is favored in play around the free-throw lane, or where the action is busy and a tall player is the receiver.

The *underhand*, or *shovel pass*, resembles a football-style lateral pass. In it the ball is thrown a short distance. It happens in situations where the handler has stopped, pivots around and feeds the ball up to a teammate who is running past.

The *baseball pass* is the "long bomb" of basketball, a quickly released one-handed throw intended to cover a fair distance. It sometimes follows a defensive rebound, with the snap throw made downcourt to start a fast break.

Shooting

The point of the game is to send a round ball through an 18-inch wide hoop that is 10 feet off the floor. To do so frequently demands a unique blend of total body movement, eye–hand coordination and timing.

The ideal shot is a unified motion that is triggered by footwork up to the fingertips, which release the ball. The ball arcs through an invisible chute down into the center of the rim as it rotates in a slow backspin.

A player's location, coverage and angle from the net determine which type of shot might be taken.

The Set Shot

In the early days of the sport, a *two-handed* set shot was the most popular way to score. The flow of the game at that time involved players getting to an open spot near the basket where they could stand steady, aim, then thrust the ball upward with both hands.

Faster action and leaping defenders, plus the fact that the two-handed set shot lacked some accuracy, led to a variation.

The *one-handed* set shot uses one hand balancing the ball to the side just above the eyes. The shooting arm almost forms

did you know?

. . . who originated the one-handed set shot?

Up until December 1936, the two-hander was standard throughout the game. (So were free throws shot underhanded!)

Then Angelo "Hank" Luisetti of Stanford showed his new shooting style in a national championship at Madison Square Garden. His one-handed baskets startled the opposition, won the game and unleashed a new approach to developing shots.

Luisetti continued to make such outstanding plays and dominated so many games that he was voted Second Best Player for the first half of the twentieth century.

a square shape from the head: the forearm is parallel with the basket, the shooting wrist bent back to be even with the upper arm and floor. The thumb and index finger are spread apart, with only the fingers and top ridge of the palm in contact with the ball.

The player takes his balanced stance: feet shoulder-width apart. His shooting forearm is lined up with the basket. He aims for the rear inside rim and springs his wrist forward, sending the ball up and away.

The follow-through leaves his fingers pointing the ball into the basket.

The Free Throw

The free throw, or foul shot, should be an automatic way to rack up points. It often plays a role in deciding which team wins, with the final score sometimes a difference between free throws made/attempted. Surprisingly, though, many players have a less-than-impressive average for scoring on free throws.

This is basically a set shot without the commotion caused by bodies moving, jumping or blocking in front. Instead players align themselves in position along each side of the free-throw lane. If not, they must stand at least six feet back from it or three feet from the circle. Players may not leave these positions or in any way hinder the free-throw shooter before the ball leaves his hands.

The shooter moves into place behind the foul line, 15 feet from the backboard, in the middle of the circle at the top of the key. This is a time to concentrate.

The best free-throw shooters follow the same pattern each time they prepare for a foul shot: step to the line, one foot slightly behind the other; get the ball from the official; maybe bounce it a few times; look at the basket; bend the knees; take a modified set shot with good follow-through.

B-Ball Basic Moves

← set shot

↑ stance

← chest pass

jump shot

layup

free
throw

41

- Rick Barry made 90 percent of the free throws he attempted—and shot them underhanded! He led the NBA for six years in free-throw accuracy. Between 1965–1980, he scored on 3,818 out of 4,243 attempts. (His all-time record percentage was surpassed in 1994 by Cleveland's Mark Price, whose career mark is .906.)
- Micheal Williams (Minnesota Timberwolves) holds the NBA record for Most Consecutive Free Throws Made. He sank 97 free throws in a row—84 at the end of the 1992–93 season and 13 more at the start of the 1993–94 campaign.

Maintaining the same, familiar approach lets the player focus more completely on his target: the rear inside rim. The one-handed set shot can be executed in a smooth, flowing motion.

One style of free throw rarely seen, if ever, is the two-handed technique shot underhanded. There is no rule against using it, but this method has been shunned by today's NBA players, who prefer the ball near eye level to better target the rim.

Many youngsters use the underhanded style when first taking up the sport. The ball is held with both hands and lowered to the knees, which are shoulder-width apart. The hands are slowly raised chest-high and forward, so that the arms are extended. The ball is let go and directed toward the net, with the hands pointing at the net in a follow-through.

The Jump Shot

The "J" gets the most use of all shots. It's a favorite because the shooter gains a sudden height advantage that lets him get off a clear shot above those in front of him.

Jump shots can occur at any point in the game. They work inside off a rebound or farther back after stopping with a pass or dribble.

Bending the knees more than he would in a basic set shot, the player springs upward as his arms bring the ball above his head. At the top of his jump, the shooting arm straightens out as a wrist snap sends the ball off the fingertips.

Classic jump shots often follow a play in which the shooter freezes an opponent by a fake pass or jab step. The sudden jump up confuses the defender as another possible fake — until the ball is released above his head.

The Hook Shot

This is a very effective surprise shot, since the player has his side or back to the basket and appears to be covered closely by a defender. But it's those same elements that make the hook shot such a beautiful move.

Using his back to protect the ball from an opponent, the player makes a quick pivot sideways. The ball is raised in his shooting hand, which swings up in a circular manner directly toward the basket.

Sometimes a jump goes along with the move, making the shot very tough to stop. The ball is released overhead in an arc above any defenders. If the shot makes a high sweeping arc it's called a "sky-hook."

did you know?

. . . who wrote the book on the sky-hook?

The classic sky-hooks made by Kareem Abdul-Jabbar remain the standard for excellence. This particular shot found the mark for many of his 15,837 field goals made: the all-time NBA record.

The Layup

A ball handler has two choices as he drives toward the net: either sneak through the defenders to rise up and lay the ball in directly or off the backboard; or before making the jump, to pass to a open teammate with a better shooting position.

In the flurry of action under the net, the fact that either move might come from a player racing in with the ball keeps opponents guessing.

The layup, or layin, begins as a power move along the floor. The player advances on an angle to the basket. His dribbling stops as the ball is brought up into the shooting hand, with his knee rising up beside it. The opposite leg pushes up off the floor. As the jump continues, the ball is gently fed to the basket, usually after it touches the backboard.

If the player delays his jump until passing the net, he does a "reverse layup." The body movement is the same, but the point of release comes under the net. The ball is delivered up backward to the rim, going in by itself or off the backboard.

The Slam Dunk

The aerial display surrounding a slam dunk thrills the fans. Of course, it's even more impressive when the home team delivers it.

The dunk is more than just a shot. It's a declaration, a way of stating, "This is *my* game right NOW!"

In its delivery, the dunk is another form of layup. The timing is critical, since there is no play off the backboard; the ball is delivered directly down through

Dunking Don'ts

- Hanging on the rim of the basket during a game, unless it is to avoid injury from falling. Penalty is a technical foul.
- Hanging on the rim during the pregame warm-up. Penalty is a $250 fine.

the hoop at the highest point of the jump. The player is not allowed to hold on to the rim unless it is to prevent injury.

Part of the excitement about the dunk is its explosive nature. It might emerge abruptly from a commotion underneath the basket, or as a conquering leap that concludes a fast break.

The Three-Point Shot

A team with outside shooters, those able to consistently sink shots from 18 feet or more beyond the basket, has a tactical advantage. While most NBA scoring is done from inside, around the net area, a series of unchallenged three-point field goals can quickly turn the tide and frustrate opponents.

The three-point field-goal line is a semicircle that arcs 22 feet away from the basket.

Three rules govern the three-pointer:

Three Points About The Three-Pointer

At first, every field goal counted for three points. Then, in 1897, it was rolled back to two points.

• • •

First introduced into the NBA for the 1979–80 season, the three-point shot originated in 1961 with the American Basketball League and was also used in the American Basketball Association between 1967–76.

• • •

Prior to the NBA's 1994–95 season, the three-point line was 23 feet 9 inches to the basket from the top of the arc, rounding to 22 feet at the corners. Now it's a uniform 22 feet.

1. the player must have at least one foot on the floor outside this line prior to the attempt;

2. the shooter may not be touching the floor on the line or be inside it;

3. only after the ball is released can the shooter touch the line or land inside the area.

Long-distance shooters got some relief with a new rule added before the 1994–95 season: a player fouled while attempting a three-point shot is awarded three free throws. If the original field goal scores, only one free throw is awarded.

A modified jump shot on the three-pointer is favored by most players, who use a short hop to help themselves power up from the floor. The trick is to always keep an eye on the basket's inside rim and not drift on the shot.

A success rate averaging 33 percent on three-point attempts is considered good, but the league leader in 1994–95, Steve Kerr of Chicago, converted better than 50 percent of his attempts.

Take Your Positions

5

Typical situation: a play begins as a defensive struggle for a rebound then suddenly becomes a fast break with a rush downcourt as players hurry to get into position. Another rebound, this time grabbed by the offense and passed around, is quickly stolen for a turnover and the action starts to swing back. . . .

Shifting from offense to defense, trying to set a play in motion or guess the opponent's next move, demands a great deal of flexibility. The need to adapt instantly to any game situation is critical.

While a player has to run, pass and shoot, each position on the court requires a particular set of skills. No team wins for individual play; championships come only through *team* play.

Playing positions used to be distinct, but the speed and action of today's NBA game sometimes require players to perform almost a part of every position. A coach has more choice in drawing his lineup.

Each floor position is given a number. The point guard is 1, the shooting guard 2, the small forward 3, the power forward

4 and the center 5. That way, there is some order to the Xs and Os drawn by the coach on those erasable boards or portable computers during timeouts at the sideline. Let's check out their roles on the court.

1 - Point Guard

An offensive march downcourt typically sees the point guard controlling the ball. He is the playmaker who directs his team's offense. The point guard does it by his excellent ball handling and passing skills. And if a shot is there to be taken, he can sink baskets, too.

He works from the "point," the section at the top of the key where a lot of action begins. A point guard sees the game as a whole: the strengths and weaknesses of all the players on the court, how they match up, who is working hard or holding back, what play can best be initiated as he crosses midcourt to do business outside the top of the key. His mastery of dribbling in tight zones, penetrating heavy traffic, allows him to scan the situation until he spies an open teammate to feed the ball to, which he does often, and very well. He breaks down defenses and gets the ball to his big men.

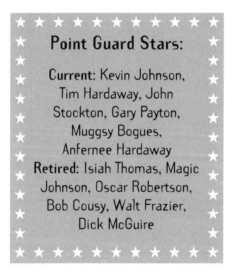

Point Guard Stars:

Current: Kevin Johnson, Tim Hardaway, John Stockton, Gary Payton, Muggsy Bogues, Anfernee Hardaway
Retired: Isiah Thomas, Magic Johnson, Oscar Robertson, Bob Cousy, Walt Frazier, Dick McGuire

Calling out the plays as he directs the movement of his team, the point guard becomes a player-coach while the game is on.

2 - Shooting Guard

The best outside shooting comes from this player, also known as the *off guard*. While the point guard organizes an attack from behind, the shooting guard makes things happen elsewhere. He might move into place to set up a screen, then quickly break loose in case he has to take the shot.

★ **Shooting Guard Stars** ★

Current: Michael Jordan, Clyde Drexler, Joe Dumars, Reggie Miller, Mitch Richmond, Jim Jackson
Retired: Jerry West, Sam Jones, Earl Monroe, Bill Sharman, George Gervin, Hal Greer

The shooting guard works with his partner, covering the middle of the court. He operates best on the wing, the area between the corner and the point. In the flow of the game he'll often switch roles with the small forward. That's why the two are sometimes referred to as swingmen.

But when the ball is delivered to his preferred location, the shooting guard is expected to hit the target.

Defense calls for guards to force turnovers by getting in on their opponents, stealing the ball before it flies past. Guards are generally better dribblers than forwards.

did you Know?

. . . Nate "Tiny" Archibald became the first guard in the NBA to convert 1,000 field goals in a season. He sank 1,028 baskets during his 1972–73 season with the Kansas City-Omaha Kings, when he led the NBA in scoring with 34.0 points per game, and also was the league's top playmaker with 11.4 assists per year. Over 13 seasons he scored a total of 16,481 points.

3 - Small Forward

The small forward moves in prime shooting range from the corner area on into the basket.

By relative standards "small" may not be the best description for players who are generally 6-6 to 6-8, or even taller. A better description might be shooting forward, a swingman who can move along with the shooting guard. Each has that keen eye to launch outside shots from his fingertips.

Besides hitting from three-point range as easily as the low post, there must be a willingness to penetrate for a layup or dig in for rebounds. The small forward is usually designated for key offensive plays, so that even without the ball he has to have good motion.

★ ★ ★ ★ ★ ★ ★ ★ ★ ★ ★ ★

Small Forward Stars

Current: Scottie Pippen, Jamal Mashburn, Glenn Robinson, Grant Hill, Glen Rice, Sean Elliott
Retired: Julius Erving, Elgin Baylor, Larry Bird, John Havlicek, Bernard King, Paul Arizin

★ ★ ★ ★ ★ ★ ★ ★ ★ ★ ★ ★

On defense, he keeps his counterpart in check by blocking shots and closing the path to the basket to prevent any drives.

4 - Power Forward

The power forward is a center, minus the height but more agile. He's physical, flexible, aggressive and in there for every rebound. It's the ideal position for an all-around player: where he can combine inside scoring with a good outside shot, dunk with delight, block shots with an arm wave, steal, screen and pass efficiently.

Around the power forward's own basket, the defensive work can be bruising as he protects his territory. It's a position he'd prefer to battle under the other hoop, the one where he can jam in that rebound he just pulled down.

5 - Center

The center is in the hub, the biggest man in a big man's game. Not only must he contend with the scrappy moves put on

him by the defense, but he also has to watch out for his own power forward going up for those jarring rebounds.

The center's presence should unnerve and distract his opponents, who will be fearful of his shot blocking and rebounding. Having a Kareem-like sky-hook or a hunger for dunking adds to the center's fearsome quality.

Few defenders can afford to turn their backs on him. When he's not playing the game in their faces, he's just bounced a pass out to an open teammate for a three-pointer.

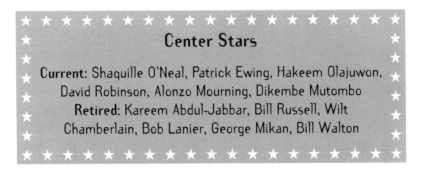

. . . centers cause rule changes?

- Until 1936, the ball would be brought to midcourt for a center jump after every basket. A rule change then allowed the team scored against to put the ball back in play with a throw-in from behind its end line.
- The first "big man" of the NBA was George Mikan of the Minneapolis Lakers. His 6-10 height would rank him a small center today, but his imprint was felt in the early 1950s: the foul lane was widened to 12 feet (from six feet) specifically to reduce his advantage.

The Sixth Man

The starting lineup of five players draws the headlines and attention. But every team is allowed to dress between eight and 12 players for a game. What about those left on the sidelines, sitting on the pine?

The game pace is so fast and fierce that substitutes are essential to relieve the starters.

The "sixth man" refers to a player who comes in off the bench when his team is lagging to give it a boost. For one of these "pine brothers," subbing may be a chance to prove that he

The Envelope, Please...

The contribution made by substitute players has been acknowledged since 1982–83 through "The Sixth Man Award," voted on by sportswriters and broadcasters.

Among the award winners have been Detlef Schrempf, Kevin McHale, Bobby Jones, Bill Walton, Ricky Pierce, Clifford Robinson and Dell Curry.

Prior to creation of the award, the NBA had many other great sixth men, notably Frank Ramsey and John Havlicek of the Boston Celtics.

deserves a move up, to be a starter himself. Others accept their role of contributing to the team with short bursts of action.

A good bench has substitutes who can step in to replace teammates on the court and can blend in with the style of play and patterns determined in countless practices. They have to be in a constant standby mode, so that when the call comes, their energy level surges.

A substitute might get in for only a few minutes per game, but his contribution is expected to maintain, if not better, the work of his replacement.

Helping It All Happen: Officials, Coaches, Trainers

6

The Officials

The game begins with an official tossing the ball up in the center jump circle. It ends when the game clock runs out as the timer blows a loud horn.

In between, all activities occur under the critical observation of an officiating crew. This includes not only the three referees in gray shirts and dark pants, but another important trio seated at a sideline table: the official scorer, the game timer and the 24-second shot clock operator.

All officials are appointed by the NBA Operations Department. During the last decade, the speed and dynamic action throughout the league grew more intense. The presence at that time of only two on-court referees became a concern for the NBA. Finally the addition of a third official, beginning in the 1988–89 season, gave the officiating crew better all-around coverage.

The referees spend their time at the edge of the spotlight, keeping the game under control while letting the players go about their own jobs without any undue disruption. But when the whistle blows and play stops, what a referee decides to judge as a wrongful action cannot be disputed.

A lot of pressure comes with the job. Success in their book means being equal and fair to both teams, so that the officiating itself does not decide the game result.

Their duties actually begin prior to the game. They must be present during the 20-minute pregame warm-up period to observe and report any infractions against the rule that prohibits hanging on the rim of the basket. It is also a chance to review timing and scoring procedures with those officials, and to ensure that the court is in proper playing condition.

When the game starts, the use of hand signals lets the referees communicate with the table personnel. These signals indicate the reasons for stopping play, the fouls called or rules violated and any penalty imposed.

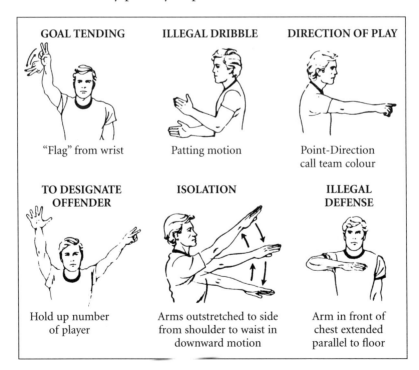

GOAL TENDING
"Flag" from wrist

ILLEGAL DRIBBLE
Patting motion

DIRECTION OF PLAY
Point-Direction call team colour

TO DESIGNATE OFFENDER
Hold up number of player

ISOLATION
Arms outstretched to side from shoulder to waist in downward motion

ILLEGAL DEFENSE
Arm in front of chest extended parallel to floor

HOLDING	**LOOSE BALL FOUL**	**ILLEGAL USE OF HANDS**

Signal foul: grasp wrist	Extended arms to shoulder level	Signal foul: strike wrist

TIME-IN	**TIME-OUT**	**PERSONAL FOUL**

Chop with hand or finger	Open palm	Clenched fist

CHARGING	**DOUBLE FOUL**	**ILLEGAL SCREEN OUT-OF-BOUNDS**

Clenched fist striking	Waving clenched fists	Arms outstretched and crossed in front of chest

20-SECOND TIME-OUT	**PUSHING**	**BLOCKING**

Hands touching shoulders	Signal foul: imitate push	Hands on hips

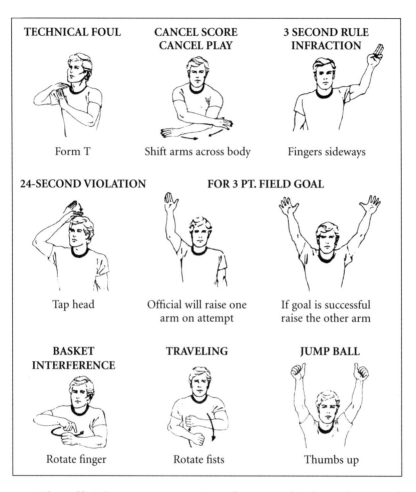

TECHNICAL FOUL	**CANCEL SCORE CANCEL PLAY**	**3 SECOND RULE INFRACTION**
Form T	Shift arms across body	Fingers sideways

24-SECOND VIOLATION	**FOR 3 PT. FIELD GOAL**	
Tap head	Official will raise one arm on attempt	If goal is successful raise the other arm

BASKET INTERFERENCE	**TRAVELING**	**JUMP BALL**
Rotate finger	Rotate fists	Thumbs up

The officials on court consist of a crew chief, a referee and an umpire.

The crew chief is the top official in charge of a game. He decides whether a goal should count if the other officials disagree, and has the final word on matters where the timers and any scorers might differ. It's also his duty to decide on rule interpretations if there is any disagreement.

During the play, an official assumes one of three positions: lead, trail or slot official. However, depending on the position of the ball on the court, these duties can overlap. The officials usually rotate positions after a foul or violation is called.

The lead official is closest to the play, and covers the front half of the court near the basket. He'll take a place along the end line to watch for fouls and violations, especially around the free-throw lane.

The trail official surveys the back part of the court and focuses on the flight of the ball to determine who scores. He can call fouls that the lead official may be unable to see.

The slot official works the area on the other side of the play, and concentrates on fouls and violations away from the ball. He hands the ball to a player on the free throw or gives a player the ball for some throw-ins from the sidelines.

As the action moves so do the officials to get the best possible view to call the play.

"This is Your Captain Speaking"

A team designates one of its players (excluding a player-coach) in uniform to be its captain. A co-captain can also be selected. This designated captain is the only player who may talk to an official during a regular or 20-second timeout charged to his team. He can "discuss" a rule interpretation, but *not* a judgment decision.

Official Scorer

Scorers record the field goals made and the free throws attempted and made, and keep a running summary of the points. They also note the personal and technical fouls, and notify the officials immediately when a sixth personal foul is called on any player.

They keep track of the timeouts charged to each team and notify an official when a team has exceeded its legal number of timeouts.

The names, numbers and positions of the players who are to start the game and those coming in as substitutions are also detailed by the scorer.

Timer

The timer operates the game clock under instructions from the officials. Whenever play begins as the result of a jump ball or a throw-in, the clock does not start until a player actually touches the ball.

The timer stops the clock for any fouls or timeouts. He is given an extra stopwatch for tracking the duration of timeouts.

If for any reason the officials are unable to establish whether a goal counted, they can ask the game timer. If he saw it score, the goal counts.

It's All in The Timing...

The game clock stops after a successful field goal:

1. in the final minute of the first three quarters;
2. in the final two minutes of the fourth quarter or overtime periods.

24-Second Clock Operator

The other official with his finger on the button is the 24-second clock operator. His duty is to start/stop/restart the timing device mounted on top of each backboard that is marked in seconds. The countdown begins when a team gains possession of the ball. The ball must be airborne on a scoring attempt within 24 seconds.

...why 24 seconds?

In the early 1950s, pro basketball was a slow game with low scoring. Once a team built up a lead, they stalled play by moving the ball in their backcourt, with endless passing that never went on the offensive.

The solution? Danny Biasone, owner of the Syracuse Nats, sensed the frustration of the fans and how they wanted the tempo of play to pick up, for the game to be filled with action.

He devised the 24-second shot clock, forcing teams to aggressively go for the basket.

How did he come up with 24 seconds?

Biasone reckoned that two teams should average 120 shots per game. He divided that number into the length of a game — 48 minutes, or 2,880 seconds — and came up with 24.

The 24-second shot clock premiered on October 30, 1954. An action-packed evening saw the Rochester Royals defeat the Boston Celtics 98–95.

The fans loved the game's new spark. Basketball had found its magic number.

The shot clock is reset to 24 seconds when one of the following occurs:

- change of possession;
- illegal defense violation;
- personal foul;
- fighting foul;
- kicking or blocking the ball with any part of the leg;
- punching the ball with a fist;
- when the ball contacts the basket ring of the team in possession of it.

If a team violates the 24-second rule, the penalty is loss of possession. The ball is handed to the defensive team for a throw-in from the boundary line closest to where play stopped.

The Coach

No person is blamed more quickly for a losing year or not given enough credit for a winning season. And in the roller coaster world of professional sports, using the phrase "a job for life" is not appropriate when speaking to a coach.

Dressed traditionally in a suit or sport jacket, he stands out along the bench where his players sit. That familiar stance, his pacing back and forth, sometimes speaking to a player or conferring with assistants, draws the fans' attention.

"No Coaches Allowed"

Dr. James Naismith and others believed that his new sport required only a referee to guide the game.

A ruling at the turn of the century decreed: "There shall be no coaching during the progress of the game by anyone connected with either of the teams." A team violating the rule had a foul shot charged against it.

How things have changed!

But they are the least of a coach's concerns. He wants to pull the best possible results out of his players. The rest of the game he tries to guess what his counterpart on the other side of the officials' table might do to win, or he urges the officials to be alert for fouls against his players or other violations by the opponents.

Today a coach in the NBA has a complex relationship with his players. He no longer can devise an intricate system, deliver it to the team and expect each player to execute it without argument. The current run-and-gun style of play changed the coach's role.

More than ever, the coach is a motivator seeking to encourage each player to achieve his full potential. Unlike baseball or football coaches, who must juggle 25- or 45-man rosters, a basketball coach deals with a dozen players regularly.

He has to make sure that his five starters get their optimum playing time; that those on the bench rotate on substitutions; that his stars get the ball a lot.

If a player is in foul trouble, the coach has to decide when best to call him off or send him back in. It's the same with timeouts. He has to judge when to use them, what strategy to suggest or whether to call a set play.

In player conflict, the coach has to draw the line ultimately and exercise discipline.

Two of The Best

Two coaches in particular represent how the role has progressed: Red Auerbach and Lenny Wilkens.

Auerbach's name is synonymous with the Boston Celtics. During his years as coach between 1950–66, the team won nine NBA Championships. He accomplished this by managing to unite a changing group of individuals throughout those years, giving each of them the desire to win. He considered himself foremost a teacher of basketball.

The influence of Arnold "Red" Auerbach continues through many of his ex-players who went on to become professional coaches themselves. They include Bob Cousy, Dave Cowens, Tom Heinsohn, K. C. Jones, Don Nelson, Frank Ramsey, Bill Russell, Tom Sanders, Bill Sharman and Paul Silas.

In January 1995, Lenny Wilkens surpassed Auerbach's coaching record of 938 wins. Wilkens was already on his way to the Hall of Fame after 15 years as a hot-shooting point guard, when he took over a full-time coaching role in 1977.

His soft-spoken patience contrasts mightily with the demeanor of some other NBA coaches. As a former player, Wilkens has empathy with those on the court. It works both ways, because his players know that he has stood in their place, felt their frustrations and achievements. Those elements of good court sense and player rapport add up to the current hiring trend that finds so many ex-players pacing the sidelines as coaches.

The NBA's All-Time Winningest Coaches

(regular-season records through 1994–95)

Coach	Won–Lost	Pct.
1. Lenny Wilkens *	969–813	.544
2. Red Auerbach	938–479	.662
3. Dick Motta	892–909	.495
4. Jack Ramsay	864–783	.525
5. Bill Fitch	862–942	.478
6. Don Nelson *	817–604	.575
7. Cotton Fitzsimmons	805–745	.519
8. Gene Shue *	784–861	.477
9. Pat Riley *	756–299	.717
10. John MacLeod	707–657	.518

* denotes coaches with NBA playing experience

The Trainer

Some aspects of the game have changed throughout the years, but one element remains constant: players get aches and pains, and there is always the potential for a serious injury.

Each NBA team employs a full-time athletic trainer to deal with players' strains from the physical grind. If specialized medical attention is required, team physicians are called in for expert advice and treatment.

Today's professional athletic trainer provides a valuable service to keep a basketball team playing in good health. The tools of his trade include ultrasound devices, electrical stimulators and other therapeutic instruments, as well as nutrition charts and, yes, ice packs. He is able to supervise injury rehabilitation programs, offer emergency care, oversee the team medical records and help to provide a stress-free environment away from the court.

The athletic trainers of every team comprise the National Basketball Trainers Association (NBTA). The group submits an extensive injury and illness report to the league each year, seeking to curb accident trends and better safeguard the players.

Most NBA athletic trainers have had experience as strength and conditioning specialists, physical therapists and/or emergency medical assistants. Through the NBTA, they spread a message of sports safety and quality health care for athletes at every competitive level.

did you Know?

• • • • • • • • • • • • • • • • • •

... the tale of the tape?
- During an average season, an NBA team uses almost 28 miles of athletic tape and wrap.
- An NBA athletic trainer can tape up a player's ankle in approximately one minute.
- Over the 82-game season, a trainer will tape almost 2,200 ankles. That's over 36 1/2 hours of continuous wrapping!

• • • • • • • • • • • • • • • • • •

Shaquille O'Neal delivers his dunk while Alonzo Mourning can only watch.

Latrell Sprewell claims air space with his slam dunk.

Where timing is everything: going for the jump ball.

A free throw attempt: will it score or rebound?

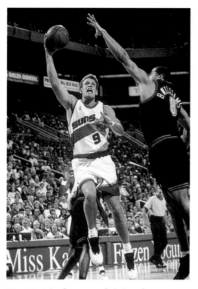

Dan Majerle on a driving layup.

Dino Radja shows perfect form with the jump shot.

Pulling down rebounds is a Dennis Rodman specialty.

When Reggie Miller blocks, Michael Jordan jumps.

Michael Jordan feeds the basket,

John Stockton controls the floor with a low dribble.

The view from above: Charles Barkley versus Hakeem Olajuwon.

The NBA's smallest player, Tyrone "Muggsy" Bogues at 5-3, is a tower of talent.

Against this looming defense, a bounce pass to the side seems like the only choice.

The defence converges outside the key.

THE NBA: YESTERDAY AND TODAY

7

Professional basketball began in 1896 when a group of players needed somewhere to play. To cover the hall rental, they charged admission that night to their game in Trenton, New Jersey. From those gate receipts, each player collected $15; the captain earned a bonus of one dollar. That started the ball not only bouncing, but "rolling."

As the sport's popularity spread, people showed a willingness to pay money to see games featuring the best players. Leagues began to form around the turn of the century, but disbanded for various reasons after a few short years. For almost the first half of this century, the professional game was divided among a number of upstart leagues with weak organizational structure. The place the sport thrived was at the college level. These young amateurs had a clean, respectable image and natural rivalries that guaranteed an audience of students, alumni and other interested sports fans for quality competition.

By the mid-1930s, Madison Square Garden regularly sold out as up to 16,000 people attended college championship matches. The public's appetite for top quality basketball had been aroused. To satisfy that hunger, a meeting was held in New York on June 6, 1946. That session created the Basketball Association of America, whose name was later changed to the National Basketball Association.

The BAA followed the design of the National Hockey League. The BAA used a hockey regular-season format that led up to a postseason playoff and championship. With five of the BAA's 11 teams operated by NHL owners (and another five with American Hockey League franchises), the game of hoops fitted neatly into their arena setting.

Besides the Knicks and the Huskies, that first season included the Boston Celtics, Cleveland Rebels, Detroit Falcons, Pittsburgh Ironmen, Providence Steamrollers, Chicago Stags, St. Louis Bombers, Washington Capitols and Philadelphia Warriors. Of those 11 original franchises, only the Knicks, Celtics and Warriors (now the Golden State Warriors) exist today.

Financial woes soon struck, the league lost a few teams and shortened its playing schedule to 48 games. What the BAA needed was something that the midwest's National Basketball League had: the country's top college players and a star attraction.

George Mikan, the NBA's first "big man."

George Mikan, a 6-10 college superstar, built the Minneapolis Lakers of the NBL into a powerhouse attraction. Size alone made Mikan a standout, but his agility and skills on the court were a marvel. His team drew sellout crowds and created fan excitement.

In 1948, Mikan and his team left the smaller NBL and joined the BAA. Five other NBL franchises soon followed, creating a 17-team league that was renamed the National Basketball Association.

The game expanded, rules were adopted to speed up the action and tempo, and a new invention called television began to take hold.

So did entrepreneurs with similar ideas. The American Basketball League (ABL) arrived in 1961 and left a year and a half later. The ABL was important for introducing the three-point shot, at a 25-foot distance from the basket.

The organizers behind the American Basketball Association (ABA) had a bit more success. Starting up in 1967, the ABA quickly made its mark using a red, white and blue basketball. The league emphasized the three-point shot and featured top stars such as Julius "Dr. J" Erving, Artis Gilmore, Moses Malone, Dan Issel and Maurice Lucas.

When the ABA dissolved in 1976, four teams — the Indiana Pacers, San Antonio Spurs, Denver Nuggets and New York (now New Jersey) Nets — were absorbed into the NBA. The remaining best players in the league were dispersed to other NBA teams.

Today the Continental Basketball Association serves as the sport's principal minor league and a proving ground for young players hoping to make it in the NBA. Known to many as "the league of dreams," the 16 teams of the CBA provide a setting where players can hone their skills. Scouts from the NBA closely follow the action and individual performances. The CBA also serves to develop future NBA officials.

Here are the current NBA teams, listed by conference and division:

The National Basketball Association

EASTERN CONFERENCE

Atlantic Division	Central Division
Boston Celtics	Atlanta Hawks
Miami Heat	Charlotte Hornets
New Jersey Nets	Chicago Bulls
New York Knicks	Cleveland Cavaliers
Orlando Magic	Detroit Pistons
Philadelphia 76ers	Indiana Pacers
Washington Bullets	Milwaukee Bucks
	Toronto Raptors

Midwest Division

Dallas Mavericks
Denver Nuggets
Houston Rockets
Minnesota Timberwolves
San Antonio Spurs
Utah Jazz
Vancouver Grizzlies

Pacific Division

Golden State Warriors
Los Angeles Lakers
Los Angeles Clippers
Phoenix Suns
Portland Trail Blazers
Sacramento Kings
Seattle SuperSonics

did you Know?

...the great pro basketball rivalry between New York and Boston began in 1946?

The New York Knicks did not win their first NBA Championship until 1970. By then the Boston Celtics had already won the NBA title *11 times!*

NBA Community Relations

The NBA recognizes its influence on the lives of so many fans, especially the young. Teams know that their success depends in large part on support from their community. That's why individual players and teams have started a number of community-relations programs. It's their way of giving something positive in return for the cheers and support.

The NBA's Stay in School Program encourages students to graduate from high school. Current and former NBA players and coaches serve as spokespeople and spread the "stay in school" message to thousands of students each year. Other efforts of this program include conflict resolution workshops that train teachers and enlighten students on how to resolve confrontations without resorting to violence, and the development of educational materials for use in the classroom.

The NBA also supports CARE, the National Committee to Prevent Child Abuse, and the Special Olympics through public service announcements and other awareness building campaigns. At the same time, players and teams across the league are involved in a number of outreach programs relating to needs of their particular communities.

The Year That Is a Season

It begins in late June each year and ends the following mid-June. For some, the NBA season never really ends.

Players always practice, coaches continue their planning, scouts search for the next hot prospect, office staff with each team and at the NBA league offices organize administrative details. Without all that behind-the-scenes activity, there would be no opening tip-off.

The Draft

This process allows teams to select the professional services of the best college players. The multimillion-dollar question on the minds of everyone in late June is "Who'll be No. 1?"

Many of those players who expect to be early picks gather in the arena for what has become the NBA event of the summer. They anxiously wait to hear which team will call out their name. Considering the thousands of players who may be eligible, just to be selected rates as an achievement. Being an early pick in the first round is outstanding. And it brings a financial windfall.

Scouting reports on a player's development are compiled through the years. Each team has its own agenda for selecting. It may be to fill a hole in its current roster or to have the option of trading that player to another team for someone else that it really prefers.

The NBA Draft focuses on the college stars, many of whom already have received national exposure in championship matches. But it is also open to a wider group.

Any person whose high-school class has graduated and is at least 17 years old can qualify for the NBA Draft *if* he renounces his intercollegiate basketball eligibility. In other words, he wants to turn professional right away. This has to be made by written notice to the NBA at least 45 days before the draft. Certain restrictions apply to teams contacting players before the draft.

The current NBA Draft involves a lottery among all the teams that failed to qualify for the playoffs the previous year. This determines the order of the first three selections in the draft. After that, the remaining teams draft according to their won–lost records, so the teams with the worst records rank highest. They get a better chance to make top selections, and hopefully not find themselves again in the basement of the league the following year.

Here's a list of the No. 1 NBA Draft picks since 1985.

YEAR	PLAYER, COLLEGE	TEAM
1985	Patrick Ewing (Georgetown)	New York Knicks
1986	Brad Daugherty (North Carolina)	Cleveland Cavaliers
1987	David Robinson (Navy)	San Antonio Spurs
1988	Danny Manning (Kansas)	Los Angeles Clippers
1989	Pervis Ellison (Louisville)	Sacramento Kings
1990	Derrick Coleman (Syracuse)	New Jersey Nets
1991	Larry Johnson (UNLV)	Charlotte Hornets
1992	Shaquille O'Neal (Louisiana State)	Orlando Magic
1993	Chris Webber (Michigan)	Orlando Magic
1994	Glenn Robinson (Purdue)	Milwaukee Bucks
1995	Joe Smith (Maryland)	Golden State Warriors

The Regular Season: 82 Games

Training camps for each team start in early October. The coaches evaluate how their players have fared since the previous season and get a chance to see their rookies in action.

Between the strength and conditioning sessions, which involve lifting weights, running and various exercises, inter-squad games are conducted. Later on the competition factor goes up a notch as NBA teams play against one another in a series of exhibition games.

Some preseason matches are held in Europe, Latin America and other parts of the world to give fans in those areas a chance to share in the NBA experience.

Decisions concerning which players will start the season are made by the coaching staff. Each team files an active list with the league office. The maximum number of active players is 12; the minimum is 11. At no time is a team permitted to dress fewer than eight players for a regular season game or nine for a playoff game. During the off-season and training camp, teams may carry as many as 20 active players.

In the first week of November, the NBA playing season officially begins. The opening tip-off will be the first of an 82-game regular season that runs until the third week of the following April.

• • • • • • • • • • • • • • • • •

did you Know?

...about the NBA in Japan?

Tokyo's Metropolitan Gymnasium bounced into athletic history in November 1990, when the Phoenix Suns went up against the Utah Jazz for the first of two matches in the Season Opening Games in Japan. The NBA became the first professional sports league to play regular season games outside North America. The NBA also sent teams to Japan for season openers in 1992 and 1994.

• • • • • • • • • • • • • • • • •

Despite the best efforts of team trainers and physical conditioners, injury or illness may be unavoidable.

When this makes a player on the roster unable to perform his duties, his name can be transferred to the injured list from the active list. A player must sit out at least five of his team's regular season games before he can return to the active list. A team can have no more than three players on its injured list at any one time.

A few other legal matters revolve around the game, which many fans will hear about but perhaps don't understand. Here they are:

The 10-Day Contract: On or after the 55th day following the first game, a team may sign a player to a 10-day contract. This can only be done to replace a player assigned to the injured list. A player can sign a maximum of two 10-day contracts with the same team.

The Trading Deadline: No trades between teams are permitted after 9 p.m. (EST) on the 16th Thursday of the regular season. From that point until the end of the regular season, player additions must be made through the waiver procedure or by signing free agents.

Waivers: A waived player is one whose contract with a team has ended and he is thus released from any obligations to that team. From August 15 to the end of the regular season, teams may claim waived players within 48 hours after notice. Players waived at any other time may be claimed within 10 days. If no team claims the waived player, he becomes a free agent. If more than one team claims a waived player, the one with the lesser record at that time gets the player. The cost for a waived player is $1,000, payable to the league.

Guaranteed Contracts: On the 56th day of the regular season, all player contracts become guaranteed for the remainder of the season.

Salary Cap: This is the amount teams may spend on player salaries, and is based on a percentage of revenues. The salary cap for the 1994–95 season was $15,964,000 per team.

The NBA All-Star Weekend

This showcase of superstars comes just in time to clear away the winter blahs. It is usually held over the second weekend of February. The NBA's best display their talents during a three-day spectacle that climaxes in the Sunday showdown.

The first NBA All-Star Game was played at Boston Garden on March 2, 1951. The East beat the West 111–94 in front of 10,094 fans. It was a landmark moment for the league in its formative years.

Now the NBA All-Star Weekend is a total happening with something for everyone even before the big game's tip-off. The event travels to a different city each year, treating local fans in the host city to a unique experience.

The NBA Jam Session presented by Fleer features exhibits, interactive activities and displays by many companies associated with the sport. Athletic clothes, equipment, training tools and fun merchandise such as trading cards and souvenirs share space alongside the interactive displays. Fans get to test their own skills against the NBA's best through shooting, dribbling and defending exercises on computerized video screens. Autograph sessions, a three-on-three tournament and lots of unexpected happenings have turned Jam Session into a highly anticipated event of its own.

★ ★ ★
ALL-STAR
WEEKEND
★ ★ ★

All-Star Saturday lets the players turn up the heat on the court. The NBA Slam-Dunk Championship features those who defy gravity with some high-flying personal touches. Past winners include Michael Jordan in 1987, who went airborne at the free throw line and stayed aloft until he stuffed the ball in the basket; and Spud Webb, whose 5-7 height rose above the competition in 1986 to prove that sometimes size isn't everything!

In the AT&T Long Distance Shootout players race against the clock from the three-point line. The league's top marksmen try to sink as many three-pointers as possible in the 24 seconds allowed. Larry Bird won his third consecutive shootout in 1988, while Craig Hodges hit 19 consecutive three-pointers to win in 1991.

All-Star Achievements:

- Kareem Abdul-Jabbar holds the record for most (18) All-Star Games played.
- Wilt Chamberlain's 42 points in 1962 rate as the top individual score in an All-Star Game. The 17 field goals he made set a record, which Michael Jordan equaled in 1988.
- Grant Hill of the Detroit Pistons became the first rookie ever to lead the fan balloting for the NBA All-Star Game. He received 1,289,585 votes for the 1995 event. Previous best showings for rookies were Magic Johnson in 1980 and Isiah Thomas in 1982, each of whom finished third.
- Magic Johnson made a one-game return from retirement in 1992, scoring 24 points with nine assists as he led the West to victory over the East 153–113. No surprise that he added the MVP award to those game-high totals.

The recent addition of the Schick Rookie Game completes the day, bringing the NBA's newest stars together in a competition that may well be the ultimate "postgraduation reunion."

But the fun is not only on the court. The weekend highlights the NBA's year-long Stay in School program. Youngsters from the host city can attend the NBA Stay in School CELEBRATION, featuring top athletic, music and TV performers. Between the entertainment and congratulations to local students, the Stay in School message comes through loud and clear.

On Sunday evening, fans around the world tune in to the showdown between the stars from the Eastern and Western Conferences. The starters are selected by fans, who vote on ballots distributed during the first half of the regular season, while the remaining All-Stars are selected by the coaches.

Ever since the initial contest in 1951, the All-Star Game has become a sky show where offense predominates. The players thrive in giving the fans what they come to see: lots of shooting. The greatest display of that was in the 1987 game, which went into overtime and had the West outscore the East 154–149. Those 303 points were the most ever scored in one All-Star Game, with Detroit's Isiah Thomas selected Most Valuable Player.

The NBA Playoffs and Finals

After a continuous trek around North America — and overseas, for several teams — on the eight-game preseason and 82-game regular season schedules, basketball's playoff rounds begin.

A total of 16 teams qualify for the NBA Playoffs. Guaranteed spots go to the four division winners. The next six teams in each conference, regardless of division, are included according to their won–lost record. The First Round is a best-of-five series. Two games at home, two away and the final back at home, if

necessary. After this, each successive round, including the NBA Finals, is a best-of-seven.

Home-court advantage in the extra game goes to the team with the better record during the regular season, regardless of the division race. For example, if a division winner plays a second-place team from another division that had a better record, the second-place team would get the home-court advantage.

To determine playoff matchups, the eight qualifiers in each conference are ranked.

The division winner with the better record becomes Team 1, the other division winner becomes Team 2 and the remaining six qualifiers are ranked Teams 3 through 8, according to their records. First Round playoff pairings are Team 1 vs. 8, 2 vs. 7, 3 vs. 6 and 4 vs. 5 in each conference. Conference Semifinals has the winner of pairing 1 and 8 play the winner of pairing 4 and 5; the victor between 2 and 7 plays the winner of 3 and 6.

The NBA Finals gives home-court advantage for the first two and last two games, if necessary, to the team with the better regular-season record. The middle three games are slotted for the opponent's home court.

NBA Playoff Structure

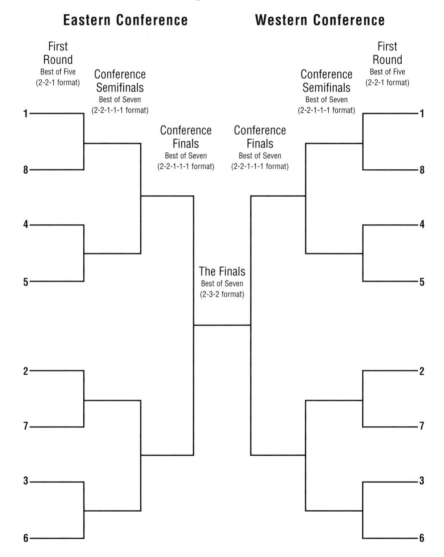

Eastern Conference

First Round
Best of Five
(2-2-1 format)

Conference Semifinals
Best of Seven
(2-2-1-1-1 format)

Conference Finals
Best of Seven
(2-2-1-1-1 format)

1
8
4
5
2
7
3
6

Western Conference

First Round
Best of Five
(2-2-1 format)

Conference Semifinals
Best of Seven
(2-2-1-1-1 format)

Conference Finals
Best of Seven
(2-2-1-1-1 format)

1
8
4
5
2
7
3
6

The Finals
Best of Seven
(2-3-2 format)

NBA Championship Facts:

- The first championship title went to the Philadelphia Warriors in 1947. The Finals against Baltimore Bullets were sold out, and the six-game series earned each Warrior about $2,000 in prize money — nearly half a season's pay for most players!

- George Mikan played with a broken hand in a cast to lead his Minneapolis Lakers to the 1949 championship over the Washington Capitols. Over the next five years, the Lakers won the title four times.

- The Boston Celtics won eight consecutive NBA Championships between 1959 and 1966. It stands as a record not only for the league, but for any professional sports team in North America.

- Boston's total of 16 NBA Championships since 1946 is the league's best. Second place overall are the Los Angeles (and formerly Minneapolis) Lakers with 11 titles.

- The Chicago Bulls' three championships in a row (1991–93) popularized a new word: "three-peat."

- Elgin Baylor's 61 points rate as the most scored in one NBA Finals game. His Los Angeles Lakers beat the Celtics 126–121 in that April 14, 1962, match.

- Michael Jordan scored 40 or more points in four consecutive games during the 1993 Finals against Phoenix Suns. His total of 246 points during the six-game series established another record.

Hoop History Highlights

9

An Aztec Tradition?

The tradition of tossing objects into targets appears to be over a thousand years old. Archaeological discoveries in Central America unearthed a very pre-Naismith version of hoops among its indigenous people.

A game known as *ollamalitzli* was reported in the 1500s by early Spanish adventurers. It involved throwing a balled-up animal skin at a round wooden fixture that had a hole in the center. Victory meant more than just winning a game: the losing team offered up one of their own as a human sacrifice!

The First Dynasty

By the turn of the century the use of substitutions was permitted, but not until 1920 was a player allowed to reenter the game. Between 1901 and 1908, the dribbler was not permitted to shoot the ball.

Basketball teams were playing in locally organized leagues or traveling the road on barnstorming tours. A team from upstate New York formed in 1895 and, known as the Buffalo Germans, became that early era's mean machine.

In a streak that made them the talk of the telegraph circuit, the Buffalo Germans won 111 consecutive games. Their wins included the 1901 Pan-Am Exposition and victories over many other pro clubs. A career won–lost record of 792–86 gave the Buffalo Germans hero status when the team retired their sweats in 1929.

The gritty style of play they and many other teams engaged in lived up to the advertising of the time, which called basketball "indoor football."

Credit for part of that comes from the scramble by players when a ball left the playing area. In those days the first team to get their hands on the ball after it went out of bounds was allowed to bring it back into play. That meant a lot of charging up stairs to the balcony, where wild tosses often landed.

A Violent Twist

Although the game was intended to exclude any physical contact, a different brand of basketball slowly emerged. Players soon began wearing special protective equipment. Padded pants, knee guards and elbow pads were used in the 1910s and 1920s during a violent period of the game's development. Players deliberately slammed into one another to fight for control of the ball, even if it meant running to the other side of the court.

This led to the need for an enclosure around the playing area so the ball could be kept in play. The preferred material was wire fencing. When assembled, it contained the court within a cagelike barrier.

The wire itself was often crudely woven, with many sharp edges sticking out. It was quite common for players to be body-checked into the barrier, and the blood flowed freely on the floor from the cuts caused by the sharp wire.

Some fans didn't make it any easier. In the halls of coal-mining towns, where the spectators brought kerosene lamps to keep away the winter chill, miners sometimes heated nails on the flame, then waited for a visiting team player to be pushed into the fence. The victim got stuck with more than just verbal abuse.

The Designated Foul Shooter

Baseball has a designated hitter who takes the pitcher's place in the American League batting order. Why shouldn't a hoop team be allowed to have a Designated Foul Shooter? In fact, they once did.

That's Why They're Called "Cagers"

The wire cage that surrounded the court to keep the ball in play and protect fans from the players, who would hurtle violently at one another, was often made of reinforced chicken wire. The cage was phased out in 1932, but the "cager" nickname persists when referring to basketball players.

A team's best free thrower would substitute in shooting from the foul line for another team member who had been fouled. But the rules were changed in 1923 to require only the player who had been fouled to take the free throw.

An Early Superstar

Leagues quickly formed to give teams a regular playing opportunity. The fans, often lured by the betting action surrounding any sort of athletic competition during this era, wanted more.

For Joe Lapchick the timing was perfect. At 6-5, he became a potent force on whatever team he played with — and he played with many. Lapchick once played in four separate games in one day — each time with a different team in a different league!

Since a center jump ball occurred after every score, Lapchick's height put him much in demand. It came at a good selling price. He'd play for a dollar a minute. The rate went to a flat fee of $50 for some games. Other times he would barter with the manager for higher rates, up to a guaranteed $100. In cases where both teams wanted his services, Lapchick auctioned himself off to the highest bidder. He finally settled into place with one team, the Original Celtics. The offer that lured him was unusual for the time: a guaranteed, regular paycheck.

The Original Celtics

The Original Celtics took the name from a defunct New York club of the 1910s, signed a few of their stars and set up home court in a Manhattan armory every Sunday night.

The team developed a zone defense that oppositions could not penetrate. Players included Nat Holman, Horse Haggerty, Swede Grimstead, Davey Banks and Pete Barry. Posters from their barnstorming treks proclaimed: "World's Basketball Champions. See the Original Pivot Play Starring The One And Only 'Dutch' Dehnert."

The Original Celtics joined a few upstart leagues for a brief time. However, the team dominated play and soon found that the financial paybacks from the leagues were much less profitable than their previous arrangements. The club went its way, earning better money for its freelance "exhibitions of excellence" on the road.

The (Original) American Basketball League

A profit was to be found in those baskets, as the Original Celtics demonstrated. A group of serious-minded businessmen decided the time was right for the game to have a league structured along the lines of baseball's enviable empire. Its postseason championship series would also be called the World Series.

The American Basketball League (ABL) began in 1925 with nine teams, including the Buffalo Germans, Boston Whirlwinds, Washington Palace 5 and Cleveland Rosenblums. Conspicuous by their absence that first season were the Original Celtics, who continued to barnstorm and earn top dollars for themselves.

What set the ABL above other early leagues were its player agreements. A team's contract to pay a regular salary also bought exclusive playing rights. No longer would a top player jump from team to team for a few dollars more.

But without a famous attraction, the ABL struggled. The life preserver came in the form of the Original Celtics. Yet a few years after they joined, the team nearly became the ABL's cement shoes.

The Original Celtics were the "Dream Team" of the late 1920s, an unstoppable group of skilled players who blanked all opponents. When the Celtics' owner landed in jail due to a swindling scandal in a separate business, the team was disbanded and its players picked up by other teams.

For a while the competition evened out and the ABL seemed as if it were here to stay. But the stock market crash of 1929 and the economic hard times that followed were too much for the new league. In 1931 the ABL finally called it quits.

The ABL legacy continues to this day in two of the rules it implemented: the three-second violation in the foul lane, and disqualification after a fifth (now sixth) personal foul.

Then Came The Rens

At the Renaissance Casino Ballroom in Harlem, Count Basie's band played during the dining and dancing. As part of the evening's entertainment, the Renaissance Five took to the floor.

Since 1922, this team played basketball at a pace that left opponents standing still. They easily could have topped the ABL standings. They proved it by beating the Original Celtics in exhibition games.

One factor prevented the "Rens" from achieving widespread success: their players were black. And in that era, black players had to keep to themselves, since they were segregated from the big leagues.

But the Rens could not contain their talents to one hall, so they took to the road. They barnstormed across the country and gathered acclaim as the premier basketball team. Between 1932 and 1936 alone they counted 473 wins in 542 games.

Outstanding teamwork became the Rens' signature. Their biggest man, "Wee Willie" Smith, and players such as Clarence "Fat" Jenkins, James "Pappy" Ricks, Charles "Tarzan" Cooper and Eyre "Bruiser" Saitch, demonstrated exceptional skills night after night, in town after town.

Their competition may have varied greatly, but the Rens knew when to rise to the occasion. One particular highlight came in 1939 with their victory over an all-star team of professionals from the new National Basketball League.

The Harlem Globetrotters

"The Clown Princes of the Court" have achieved such popularity that even those who know nothing else about basketball may have seen the troupe perform. In the 1970s a TV cartoon series aired, based on their comic adventures and routines, which have become familiar all around the world.

But in 1927, when the Savoy 5 were first seen in the ballroom of Chicago's Savoy Hotel, they played between dance bands as part of an entertainment package.

Abe Saperstein, a small but spirited player himself, saw potential. He offered to manage the Savoy 5, outfitted them in patriotic red, white and blue uniforms and gave them a new name: the Harlem Globetrotters.

Although it would be another 40 years before they actually played in Harlem, the Globetrotters did circle the world several times before then.

From the beginning, they were a serious team going up against the other barnstormers of the day. They played the Rens in hard competitions — which they sometimes won, beat the Original Celtics and showed professional teams a few new things about the game. The more familiar, comic side of the Globetrotters emerged from the pregame warm-ups and half-time breaks when the players would be having fun with one another. These sessions grew longer and became more amusing. Soon that's what the public paid very well to see.

The best routines of the Globetrotters (placekicking a ball from center court into the basket, boosting a player onto the shoulders to let him score, tossing a bucket of confetti into the crowd, losing the ball under someone's shirt) are legend. What also became obvious was their skillful dribbling, passing and shooting. The exercises done to the song "Sweet Georgia Brown" showed a magician-like touch with a basketball.

The champion Minneapolis Lakers discovered more than just amusing stunts one night during an exhibition game in 1949 when they lost soundly to the Globetrotters.

Stars with the 'Trotters since then include Marques Haynes and "Goose" Tatum. Later Meadowlark Lemon and Curly Neal became the leading attractions. And for one year after leaving college and before joining the NBA, Wilt Chamberlain was a Globetrotter. Today the troupe continues to travel the world, spreading their news about the fun side of the game. And still astounding audiences everywhere.

The National Basketball League

The experience of the ABL left the future of pro basketball uncertain. Audiences would show up to see traveling barnstormers take on local competition, and the colleges always had their own interested fans, but the matter of whether a pro league could survive kept coming back.

In 1937, with sponsorship money coming from some of the big industries at the time, the National Basketball League started up. Companies like Firestone, General Motors and Goodyear supported teams and sometimes threw in a contract inducement offering work after one's playing days were over. With the only other option being to barnstorm, the NBL was difficult to resist. An available talent pool of ex-college players stocked the franchises.

While the organization itself was shoddy, and many scheduling oversights led to an uneven way of assessing winners and losers, the league plodded on.

Now-familiar rules took hold: the 10-second violation forced players to move the ball over the center line, and the center jump ball after each basket was discontinued.

World War II arrived and basketball took a back seat to history. Many players went off to enlist and the dwindling franchises struggled to stay afloat.

That's perhaps one reason the Fort Wayne Zollner Pistons went to the finals in their first season of play. The team entered the league in 1941 under the sponsorship of Fred Zollner, whose piston manufacturing business gave him the resources to support a club. The Pistons began a legacy of pro ball in the area, which continues today in their ongoing existence as the Detroit Pistons.

By the time giant George Mikan entered the NBL, the league appeared to have a real chance for expanding beyond its Midwest base. However, that possibility ended with the formation in New York of the Basketball Association of America.

After several franchises took up an offer to join the BAA in 1949, the NBL folded.

And thus came the NBA.

Breaking The Color Bar

Something about the early days of pro basketball is obvious from photographs taken at the time: all the players were white. Segregation in American society may have been slowly peeling away, but in sports the color bar continued. Jackie Robinson's entry into baseball changed the course of history.

For basketball, the matter was never a case of "What?" but "When?" As barnstorming teams like the Rens and the Globetrotters proved, the sport had to confront reality; to see people for their abilities, not their skin color.

By excluding African Americans for so long, the athletic world deprived many great athletes of proper recognition, as

Raising The Hoop

On March 7, 1954, the NBA raised the hoops for one game from 10 feet to 12 feet off the floor. The extra elevation was an experiment to remove the height advantage enjoyed by the league's 6-10 superstar, George Mikan.

His Minneapolis Lakers still beat the Milwaukee Hawks, with Mikan having another great night.

The experiment was ended as people realized that Mikan's height continued to give him the edge. The hoops were lowered back to 10 feet and have remained there since.

well as due financial reward. In the NBA, the color bar finally came down in 1950, the league's fourth season.

That spring, Boston Celtics owner Walter Brown drafted Chuck Cooper. The Washington Capitols later drafted Earl Lloyd, and weeks later the New York Knicks signed Harlem Globetrotter sensation Nat "Sweetwater" Clifton.

As for who actually became the first black player to take to the court in the NBA, the 1950–51 league schedule gave that distinction to Earl Lloyd, whose Capitols began the season one day before the Celtics and five days before the Knicks.

The World's Game

FIBA — Fédération Internationale de Basketball

Dr. James Naismith's colleagues of the YMCA Training School brought his invention around the world. Basketball was played in Mexico in 1892, a year after being invented. By 1894 the game was in China and India; the following year, in England. The sport expanded into Russia in 1905, Italy in 1907, Greece by 1919. Wherever graduates of the Springfield YMCA went, the new game followed along as standard recreation.

Along with its sudden growth, the interpretation of rules varied greatly. Finally three faculty members of the International YMCA School of Physical Education in Switzerland met to coordinate the rules of the increasingly global game.

In 1932 they formed the *Fédération Internationale de Basketball*, known as FIBA. Standardizing the rules for international play allowed countries to play one another without multiple meetings before a game, which had been the case.

FIBA's efforts led to the sport's being adopted into the Olympic Games just four years later.

Today FIBA remains the sport's international governing body. It conducts many global events, including the World Championship of Basketball, held every four years and contested by national teams.

The 1994 World Championship in Toronto marked the first time the games were held in North America. A total of 120 national teams began playing elimination games over a year before the tournament. The 16 best men's teams met for the final competitions, which were televised to over 80 countries on all five continents, reaching an estimated audience of 1.8 billion viewers.

What they saw was the first FIBA World Championship to permit the entry of NBA players, whose professional status had previously excluded them from competition. And that seemed like a replay of what the world had seen at the 1992 Summer Olympics in Barcelona.

The Olympics

"The Dream Is Alive" became the rallying cry of pro basketball fans when FIBA changed its policy on amateur status in 1989. At last players from the National Basketball Association would be allowed to represent their countries in the Olympic Games. No longer would the best be made to rest!

Once the roster for the USA basketball team was announced, the incredible lineup of talent took on the nickname "Dream Team." Not just fans of the NBA tuned in; Dream Fever captured the world's attention.

The games in Barcelona showed an awesome display of basketball skills, not only to spectators but even to the other competitors. The Dream Team simply raised the game to a new level. A gold medal was never in doubt. The key question was, just how would they do it? The whole world was watching. And loved what it saw.

The 1992 USA Olympic Men's Basketball Team (i.e., The Dream Team)

(Gold Medal, Olympics, Barcelona)

Charles Barkley	Phoenix Suns
Larry Bird	Boston Celtics
Clyde Drexler	Portland Trail Blazers
Patrick Ewing	New York Knicks
Earvin "Magic" Johnson	Los Angeles Lakers
Michael Jordan	Chicago Bulls
Christian Laettner	Minnesota Timberwolves
Karl Malone	Utah Jazz
Chris Mullin	Golden State Warriors
Scottie Pippen	Chicago Bulls
David Robinson	San Antonio Spurs
John Stockton	Utah Jazz
Chuck Daly (coach)	Detroit Pistons

Dream Team II

(Gold Medal, 1994 FIBA World Championship, Toronto)

Derrick Coleman	New Jersey Nets
Joe Dumars	Detroit Pistons
Tim Hardaway *	Golden State Warriors
Kevin Johnson	Phoenix Suns
Larry Johnson	Charlotte Hornets
Shawn Kemp	Seattle SuperSonics
Dan Majerle	Phoenix Suns
Reggie Miller	Indiana Pacers
Alonzo Mourning	Charlotte Hornets
Shaquille O'Neal	Orlando Magic
Mark Price	Cleveland Cavaliers
Steve Smith	Miami Heat
Isiah Thomas *	Detroit Pistons
Dominique Wilkins	Los Angeles Clippers
Don Nelson (Coach)	Golden State Warriors

(* named to team, but due to injury in 1993 94 NBA season, did not play)

Yes, They Do It All!

Before the '92 Olympics, the NBA had been limited to playing foreign teams in the McDonald's Championship. This is a FIBA-sanctioned event held annually from 1987 to 1991 and semiannually since then (in years when there is no Olympics or World Championship). In its present format, the defending NBA champion plays in a tournament format against top international clubs, champions in their respective leagues. The NBA team has won each year.

The McDonald's Championship presented a working opportunity for the NBA. Some recent rule changes in the league (shortening the three-point line, awarding three free throws to a shooter fouled during a three-point attempt) had already been instituted by FIBA, the sport's governing body.

Adapting those regulations is significant in that it shows movement toward standardizing the playing rules across the world, to assist in the expanding growth of basketball.

Key Points in Hoop History

- 1891 - "Basket ball" invented by Dr. James Naismith in Springfield, Massachusetts.
- 1892 - First public game: Naismith's students defeat the teachers.
- 1893 - The pivot is no longer a traveling violation.
- 1894 - The free throw is introduced, valued at one point.
- 1895 - Backboards required; also, the five-man team becomes standard, down from the nine-man team that Naismith originally planned.
- 1896 - First professional game, Trenton, New Jersey.
- 1898 - The double dribble prohibited.
- 1898 - First pro league: National Basketball League starts with teams from New Jersey, New York and Pennsylvania, but disbands after two years.

- 1900 - Substitutions allowed, but player cannot reenter game.
- 1901 - The Buffalo Germans form the first dynasty, with 111 consecutive wins in a three-year period.
- 1904 - Olympic Games in St. Louis: basketball is played as a demonstration sport.
- 1915 - The New York "Original Celtics" begin, a powerhouse until the late 1930s.
- 1920 - Substituted player allowed to re-enter game.
- 1921 - "Basket ball" now formally written as "basketball."
- 1922 - The New York Renaissance 5 (the Rens) begin their 18-year reign.
- 1924 - Designated foul shooter prohibited: free throw now must be taken by player fouled.
- 1926-31 - American Basketball League operates.
- 1927 - Harlem Globetrotters formed as competitive barn-storming club.
- 1932 - Ten-second violation for not moving ball across center line.
- 1932 - Fédération Internationale de Basketball (FIBA) organized.
- 1936 - Olympic Games in Berlin: basketball becomes a medal sport.
- 1936 - The center jump ball after every basket is eliminated; ball now thrown in by the defensive team.
- 1936 - Hank Luisetti introduces one-handed set shot.
- 1939 - New York Rens win 112 games, take world title.
- 1940 - Television discovers basketball: a college game at Madison Square Garden is shown on local TV.
- 1946 - Basketball Association of America starts with 11 teams. First game played at Maple Leaf Gardens, Toronto.
- 1949 - BAA + NBL = NBA (the survivors from the National Basketball League join the Basketball Association of America, which changes its name to the National Basketball Association).

- 1950 - Boston Celtics draft Chuck Cooper, the Washington Capitols draft Earl Lloyd and the New York Knicks sign Nat "Sweetwater" Clifton; a quirk in the schedule makes Lloyd the first black player to appear in an NBA game.
- 1950 - Fort Wayne Pistons beat Minneapolis Lakers 19–18 in the NBA's lowest scoring game.
- 1951 - First NBA All-Star Game, Boston Garden.
- 1952 - NBA foul lane is widened to 12 feet (from 6 feet).
- 1954 - The 24-second shot clock is introduced; a free throw is awarded after the opposing team's fifth foul in any quarter.
- 1959 - Boston Celtics win first of eight consecutive NBA titles.
- 1960 - NBA moves west: Minneapolis Lakers relocate to become Los Angeles Lakers.
- 1962 - Wilt Chamberlain scores 100 points in a game.
- 1964 - NBA foul lane is widened to 16 feet (from 12 feet).
- 1966 - Boston Celtics win their eighth consecutive NBA title.
- 1967 - American Basketball Association (ABA) starts play.
- 1968 - Naismith Memorial Basketball Hall of Fame opens on campus in Springfield, Massachusetts.
- 1970 - NBA expands to 17 teams.
- 1972 - Los Angeles Lakers win 33 games in a row.
- 1974 - Moses Malone signs with ABA, first player in modern era to turn pro directly out of high school.
- 1976 - ABA folds, but four of its teams join NBA.
- 1979 - Three-point shot from beyond 23 feet 9 inches introduced to NBA.
- 1985 - Naismith Memorial Basketball Hall of Fame relocates to permanent home in downtown Springfield.
- 1986 - Boston Celtics end season with 40–1 home win record.
- 1987 - NBA expands to 27 teams.
- 1987 - McDonald's Championship, Milwaukee: first FIBA-sanctioned event with NBA participation.

Basketball 'n' Baseball

Michael Jordan made it most obvious: there is an allure between hoops and home runs. When the Chicago Bulls superstar retired temporarily from the game in 1993, he did so to follow his dream of becoming a baseball player. Even if that meant riding the buses in the minor leagues.

For Danny Ainge, it was the other way around. He left third base with the Toronto Blue Jays in 1981 to join the Boston Celtics.

Dave DeBusschere, a basketball Hall of Famer, helped the New York Knicks to NBA titles in 1970 and 1973, following his career as a pitcher with the Chicago White Sox in 1962–63. And Gene Conley won championships in both sports — as a forward with the Boston Celtics in 1959, 1960 and 1961, and as a pitcher with the Milwaukee Braves in 1957.

Other baseball players have been drafted by NBA teams, but chose not to leave their field of dreams.

Longtime baseball star Dave Winfield was drafted by the Atlanta Hawks in 1973, and when the Clippers were in San Diego in 1981, they chose outfielder Tony Gwynn of the San Diego Padres.

- 1988 - Atlanta Hawks become first NBA team to play in Russia, playing a series of exhibitions.
- 1988 - NBA reintroduces system of three officials working a game (originally tried in 1978–79).
- 1990 - Utah Jazz vs. Phoenix Suns in Tokyo, Japan: NBA becomes first pro sports league to play regular season games outside of North America.
- 1992 - Olympic Games in Barcelona: Dream Team wins gold.

- 1993 - Chicago Bulls three-peat, becoming first NBA team in 27 years to win three consecutive titles.
- 1994 - FIBA World Championship of Basketball in Toronto: Dream Team II takes gold.
- 1995 - Toronto and Vancouver begin play in NBA, the first international expansion teams. There are now 29 teams in the league.

Love Those Numbers!

The scores always total in the hundreds; assists are credited for rapid passes that lead to goals; the fastest arms grab the rebounds; a dunk can get a basket as sure as a 20-foot jumper; substitutions come and go; everyone commits a foul sometime; and the clock counts down in tenths of seconds. Out of all the action on the court, a set of numbers emerges that details the performance. The stats, please.

If it were not for the Official Scorer at the courtside table, the referees might not know which player fouled out; a team might be unaware that its opponents had only one timeout remaining; the fans would be left wondering how many assists or points a player made during the game and how many he attempted.

Keeping Track of The Score

Statistics from a basketball game originate from the Official Scorer's Report. The details are compiled instantly on a courtside computer program, developed specifically for the NBA.

Boston Celtics at CLEVELAND CAVALIERS   4TH QUARTER
04/04/1995 Gund Arena - Cleveland, OH
CAVALIERS Starters: Mills Cage Williams Brandon Campbell
Celtics Starters: McDaniel Radja Ellison Douglas Wilkins

Time	CAVALIERS	Score	Lead	Celtics
12:00		Start of Quarter (9:16 PM)		
12:00	Possession: Cavaliers	73-68	+5	
11:46	Brandon 1FT (GOOD)	74-68	+6	Celtics T.FOUL (Illegal Defense)
11:32	Campbell 2FT (GOOD, GOOD)	76-68	+8	Wilkins (P1,T1) S.FOUL
11:16		76-70	+6	Wilkins DRIVING LAYUP
11:16	Campbell (P1,T1) S.FOUL			
11:16	SUB: FERRY FOR MILLS			
11:16				Wilkins 1FT (MISS)
10:43	Williams (P4,T2) P.FOUL			
10:43	SUB: HILL FOR WILLIAMS			
10:24		76-72	+4	Douglas LAYUP
09:57	Hill 8' HOOK	78-72	+6	
09:39	Cage (P2,T3) P.FOUL			
09:39				SUB: MONTROSS FOR ELLISON
09:32	Hill (P4,T4) S.FOUL	78-74	+4	Montross 2FT (GOOD, GOOD)
08:50	Ferry TRAVELING TO #12			
08:38	Cage (P3,PN) S.FOUL	78-76	+2	Montross 2FT (GOOD, GOOD)
08:09	Campbell 3 PT 24' JUMP (Hill)	81-76	+5	
07:53		81-78	+3	Douglas DRIVING LAYUP
07:50	20 SEC TIMEOUT			
07:50	TIMEOUT (4)			
07:50	SUB: PHILLS FOR FERRY			
07:50	SUB: PRICE FOR BRANDON			
07:41	Campbell 16' JUMP (Price)	83-78	+5	
07:07	Hill BAD PASS TO #13			
06:45	Phills TRAVELING TO #14			
06:27				Radja 3 SEC VIOLATION TO #10
06:27				SUB: BROWN FOR MCDANIEL
06:12	Campbell 16' JUMP (Price)	85-78	+7	
06:10				TIMEOUT (4)
06:10	SUB: WILLIAMS FOR CAGE			
05:55	STEAL Williams			
05:53				Radja (P4,T2) P.FOUL
05:06		85-80	+5	Douglas DRIVING LAYUP
04:33				TIMEOUT (5)
04:21		85-82	+3	Douglas DRIVING LAYUP
04:04				Wilkins (P2,T3) P.FOUL
03:55	SUB: MILLS FOR CAMPBELL			
03:44		85-84	+1	Douglas DRIVING LAYUP
03:24	Price BAD PASS TO #15			STEAL Douglas
03:19		85-86	-1*	Radja FB DRIVING DUNK (Brown)
03:15	TIMEOUT (5)			
02:34		85-88	-3	Wilkins TIP
01:24	Hill (P5,PN) P.FOUL	85-90	-5	Radja 2FT (GOOD, GOOD)
01:15	Phills LAYUP (Price)	87-90	-3	
01:01				Brown OUT OF BOUNDS TO #12
:50.7	Hill (P6,PN) P.FOUL			
:50.7	SUB: CAGE FOR HILL			
:50.7		87-91	-4	Wilkins 2FT (GOOD, MISS)
:49.5	TIMEOUT (6)			
:49.5	SUB: FERRY FOR CAGE			
:49.5				SUB: STRONG FOR MONTROSS
:35.7	Williams (P5,PN) P.FOUL	87-93	-6	Brown 2FT (GOOD, GOOD)
:29.5				Douglas (P2,T4) P.FOUL
:23.7	Ferry DRIVING LAYUP	89-93	-4	
:22.3	Wiliams (P6,PN) P.FOUL			
:22.3	SUB: ROBERTS FOR WILLIAMS			
:22.3		89-95	-6	Brown 2FT (GOOD, GOOD)
:10.8	Mills 2FT (MISS, GOOD)	90-95	-5	Wilkins (P3,PN) L.B. FOUL
:07.9	Mills (P3,PN) P.FOUL	90-97	-7	Brown 2FT (GOOD, GOOD)
:00.9	Mills 6' RUNNING JUMP	92-97	-5	

End of 4th Quarter (19-29)
End of Quarter (9:51 PM)

BIG HOME LEAD 8			*LEAD CHANGES 1
BIG VISITOR LEAD 7			TIMES TIED 0
4 FOR 4 PTS			3 FOR 2 PTS
7/20 for 35.0%		FIELD GOALS	8/17 FOR 47.1%
4/5 FOR 80.0%		FREE THROWS	13/15 FOR 86.7%
OFF: 2 DEF: 6		REBOUNDS	OFF: 3 DEF: 7
Campbell: 9		HIGH SCORER	Douglas: 10
Hill: 3		HIGH REBOUNDER	Wilkins: 4
Price: 3		HIGH ASSISTS	Brown: 1

The entire event that comprises one quarter of a game is detailed on a running stat sheet according to the minute and second, and what the score was at that moment. This short-hand description forms the basis of what a newspaper reader might find in the sports pages the next day. The running score sheet is an accurate summary of what took place and is used by the media to help them with their game stories.

Look closely at the play-by-play report for the fourth quarter of a Celtics-Cavaliers game. Up top are the details of which teams played, when and where. The names of the starting players for the quarter are listed. The "real time" *(9:16 PM)* is included to show the start of the period.

Next, each line describes what occurred at a particular moment.

Let's focus on the game report with *5:06* left in the quarter.

The score shows *85* for Cleveland Cavaliers and *80* for the Boston Celtics. Cavaliers had the lead by 5 points *(+5)* when the Celtics' Sherman Douglas scored on a layup: *Douglas DRIVING LAYUP.*

Play continued until there was *4:33* left in the quarter and the Celtics called a *TIMEOUT (5),* their fifth of the game. Whatever strategy they discussed seemed to have worked out, because just 12 seconds later when the clock ticked down to *4:21,* the Celtics brought the score to *85–82,* cutting the Cavaliers lead down to 3 points *(+3)* on another *Douglas DRIVING LAYUP.*

At *4:04,* Dominique Wilkins was called for a personal foul: *Wilkins (P2,T3) P.FOUL.* The report shows it was his second personal foul, and Boston's third team foul for that quarter.

A substitution was made by the Cavs when Chris Mills replaced Tony Campbell at *3:55* as shown by *SUB: MILLS FOR CAMPBELL.*

That didn't stop Boston's momentum, because with *3:44* left, the score became *85–84* as the Cavs' lead was shaved to *+1* with yet another *Douglas DRIVING LAYUP.*

At the *3:24* point, a mistake occurred when Cleveland tried moving the ball. *Price BAD PASS TO#15* tells us that Mark Price made a bad pass which was the Cavs' fifteenth turnover of the game. The note at the right side of the page reports *STEAL Douglas* to show that Sherman Douglas stole the ball from Price.

That move must have ignited the Celtics, because five seconds later with *3:19* left, the score changed to *85–86* favoring Boston, as *-1** indicates the change in lead. It happened with Dee Brown passing the ball on a fast break to Dino Radja who scored on a dunk: *Radja FB DRIVING DUNK (Brown).*

Four seconds later, at *3:15*, the Cavaliers called *TIMEOUT (5),* their fifth of the Game, to regroup and try to stop the Celtics' scoring surge.

Play resumed, but at *2:34* the Boston streak continued with Wilkins jumping up under the Cavs net to get two points on a tip-in. The *Wilkins TIP* made the score *85–88*, with the Cleveland lead still in the negative numbers, *-3*.

At *1:24*, Cleveland's Tyrone Hill committed a personal foul on Dino Radja. Indicated by *Hill (P5,PN) P.FOUL*, the official scorer reports it was Hill's fifth personal foul *(P5)*, and his team was in the Penalty Situation *(PN)*. That sent Radja to the free throw line with a bonus foul shot; he scored on both the first and second attempt: *Radja 2FT (GOOD, GOOD).* That raised the score to 85–90.

The drought for Cleveland ended with *1:15* left, on a Mark Price pass to Bobby Phills who went in for two points: *Phills LAYUP (Price).* That was nearly five minutes after their last basket, a jump shot from sixteen feet by Tony Campbell with an assist by Mark Price: *6:12 Campbell 16' JUMP (Price).*

All that describes what took place in just five minutes during this particular game. What the score sheet can't tell is how the players on the court reacted at *11:46* when the Celtics were given a technical foul for illegal defense: *Celtics T.FOUL (Illegal*

Defense), which sent Terrell Brandon to the free throw line to sink a basket: *Brandon 1FT (GOOD)*; what the coaches were doing on the sidelines with *7:50* remaining during the consecutive timeouts called by Cleveland, the first for twenty seconds: *20 SEC TIMEOUT* followed by a regular timeout of one minute and forty seconds *TIMEOUT (4)*, their fourth; how the fans yelled at *8:09* reacting to Campbell's 3-point jump shot from 24 feet out: *Campbell 3 PT 24' JUMP (Hill)* which kept the Cavs leading at that point *81–76*; during the pauses, what music was pounding. In other words, the rest of the surrounding excitement of an NBA game.

With less than one second *(:00.9)* in the game, Chris Mills made the final scoring play on a running jump shot from six feet out: *Mills 6' RUNNING JUMP*.

The rest of the fourth quarter report tell us how many points each team scored *(19–29)* and that the period ended at *9:51 PM*, then lists the scoring percentages and team leaders for those 12 minutes of play.

• • • • • • • • • • • • • • • • •

• • • • • • • • • • • • • • • • •

Individual Statistics

Based on the Official Scorer's report, a game's statistics for each individual are compiled.

04/04/1995 Gund Arena - Cleveland, OH
Officials: #35 Jack Nies, #07 Bernie Fryer, #59 Mike Smith

Time of Game: 2:11
Attendance: 20,562

VISITOR: Boston Celtics (30-43)

NO	PLAYER		MIN	FG	FGA	3P	3PA	FT	FTA	OR	DR	TOT	A	PF	ST	TO	BS	PTS
12	Dominique WILKINS	F	37	4	18	0	4	3	7	3	6	9	2	3	0	0	0	11
31	Derek STRONG	F	13	0	5	0	0	4	4	1	3	4	0	0	0	0	0	4
00	Eric MONTROSS	C	30	2	4	0	0	4	4	4	5	9	0	2	1	2	0	8
20	Sherman DOUGLAS	G	43	11	21	0	1	2	2	1	1	2	6	2	1	2	0	24
07	Dee BROWN	G	35	3	11	0	2	9	9	1	3	4	6	4	3	3	0	15
29	Pervis ELLISON		17	3	5	0	0	0	0	3	2	5	0	3	0	0	0	6
40	Dino RADJA		36	8	17	0	0	7	8	2	4	6	2	4	1	3	0	23
09	Greg MINOR		9	0	0	0	0	0	0	0	1	1	1	3	0	0	0	0
34	Xavier MCDANIEL		20	2	5	0	0	2	2	1	4	5	1	1	1	1	1	6
05	Jay HUMPHRIES		DNP - Coach's Decision															
45	Tony DAWSON		DNP - Coach's Decision															
55	Acie EARL		DNP - Coach's Decision															
	TOTALS:		240	33	86	0	7	31	36	16	29	45	18	22	7	11	1	97

PERCENTAGES: 38.4%   0.0%   86.1%   TM REB: 13   TOT TO: 12 (11 PTS)

HOME: CLEVELAND CAVALIERS (39-33)

NO	PLAYER		MIN	FG	FGA	3P	3PA	FT	FTA	OR	DR	TOT	A	PF	ST	TO	BS	PTS
24	Chris MILLS	F	35	4	7	0	1	1	2	0	2	2	2	3	0	0	1	9
32	Tyrone HILL	F	39	5	8	0	0	2	5	2	7	9	2	6	1	3	0	12
18	John WILLIAMS	C	36	6	13	0	0	3	5	0	6	6	1	6	1	5	3	15
25	Mark PRICE	G	32	4	13	1	5	6	7	0	3	3	14	1	1	3	0	15
14	Bobby PHILLS	G	37	6	11	0	1	5	5	0	7	7	1	3	1	2	1	17
11	Terrell BRANDON		16	3	7	0	0	1	1	1	1	2	4	1	0	0	0	7
44	Michael CAGE		19	0	1	0	0	0	0	0	3	3	0	3	0	0	0	0
35	Danny FERRY		10	1	4	0	0	0	0	1	0	1	1	0	0	1	0	2
09	Tony CAMPBELL		15	4	6	1	1	6	6	0	1	1	0	1	0	0	0	15
31	Fred ROBERTS		1	0	0	0	0	0	0	0	0	0	0	0	0	0	0	0
05	Steve COLTER		DNP - Coach's Decision															
30	Greg DREILING		DNP - Coach's Decision															
	TOTALS:		240	33	70	2	9	24	31	4	30	34	25	24	4	14	6	92

PERCENTAGES: 47.1%   22.2%   77.4%   TM REB: 10   TOT TO: 15 (12 PTS)

SCORE BY PERIODS	1	2	3	4	FINAL
Celtics	18	28	22	29	97
CAVALIERS	27	24	22	19	92

Technical Fouls - Individual
  Celtics: NONE
  CAVALIERS (1): 1:39 2nd Williams

Technical Fouls - Illegal Defense
  Celtics (1): 11:46 4th Celtics
  CAVALIERS: NONE

Total Illegal Defenses: Celtics 2, CAVALIERS 0
Points in the Paint: Celtics 54, CAVALIERS 32
Second Chance Points: Celtics 14, CAVALIERS 3
Fast Break Points: Celtics 4, CAVALIERS 4

MEMO: Tonight's sellout (20,562) was the CAVS' 27th of the season (franchise record).
MEMO: Tonight's sellout was also the CAVS' 13th in a row (also a franchise record).

The date, place, length of game, referees, and attendance are listed along the top. The win/loss record shows the Visitors, Boston, now have 30 wins to their 43 losses for the season. Let's examine how Boston's Sherman Douglas did during the game, so that we can decipher the initials on the line above.

Sherman Douglas wears number *(NO)* 20. He played 43 minutes *(MIN)* of the game and scored on 11 field goals *(FG)*, of his 21 field goals attempted *(FGA)*. He did not succeed on the 3-point shot *(3P)*, of the one 3-pointer attempted *(3PA)*. Taking foul shots, he scored on 2 free throws *(FT)* of the 2 free throws he attempted *(FTA)*.

Under the baskets, he got inside the Cavs to grab 1 offensive rebound *(OR)* and helped his team out by pulling down 1 defensive rebound *(DR)* below his own net, for a *(TOT)* total of 2 rebounds. He passed six times to teammates which directly led to a field goal, counting up 6 assists *(A)*.

Douglas committed 2 personal fouls *(PF)*, made 1 steal *(S)* of the ball from the Cavs, but lost the ball to them on 2 turnovers *(TO)*. He didn't block any shots *(BS)*.

Altogether in the game, he scored a total of 24 points *(PTS)*.

The team totals and percentages for each category are listed underneath. As well, even though they dressed for the game and were on the bench, a few players did not play *(DNP)*, due to a *COACH'S DECISION.*

did you Know?

...who scored the most points in one NBA game?

Superstar center Wilt Chamberlain. He did it the night he became the first — and only — NBA player to score 100 points in a game.

The New York Knicks were the victims of this March massacre in 1962, losing 169–147 to the Philadelphia Warriors at Hershey Arena.

Deciphering a Box Score

The results of a game between the Detroit Pistons and the San Antonio Spurs let you decipher the kind of box score seen most often in the daily newspapers.

PISTONS 97 at SPURS 114

DETROIT (97)
    Miller 4-9 0-0 8, Hill 4-13 1-4 9, West 3-6 3-4 9, Dumars 13-25 5-6 34, Houston 7-14 0-0 19, Addison 5-11 4-4 16, Curley 1-1 0-0 2, Macon 0-0 0-0 0, Knight 0-1 0-0 0, Leckner 0-1 0-0 0. Totals 37-81 13-18 97.
SAN ANTONIO (114)
    Rodman 2-3 2-2 6, Elliott 6-11 9-9 24, Robinson 11-18 15-23 37, Johnson 3-10 1-2 7, Del Negro 6-11 3-3 15, Person 2-7 0-0 5, Rivers 3-7 2-2 8, Cummings 1-3 1-2 3, Reid 2-4 2-2 6, Anderson 0-0 0-0 0, Haley 1-3 0-2 2. Totals 37-77 35-47 114.

Detroit	28	25	28	16— 97
San Antonio	27	27	32	28—114

    3-Point goals—Detroit 10-20 (Dumars 3-7, Houston 5-10, Addison 2-3), San Antonio 5-15 (Elliott 3-7, Del Negro 0-1, Person 2-6, Rivers 0-1). Fouled out—West. Rebounds—Detroit 45 (Miller 10), San Antonio 56 (Rodman 21). Assists—Detroit 21 (Hill 11), San Antonio 26 (Johnson 8). Total fouls—Detroit 31, San Antonio 19. Technicals—Rodman, Miller. Ejections—Miller. A—20,443 (20,662).

To find out what Pistons star Joe Dumars did that night, look at his numbers in the Detroit listing:

Dumars 13–25 5–6 34

The first set denotes TOTAL FIELD GOALS MADE/ ATTEMPTED: he sank 13 of his 25 shots.

The second set lists TOTAL FREE THROWS MADE/ ATTEMPTED: Dumars sank 5 of the 6 foul shots he was awarded.

The final number shows his TOTAL POINTS scored was 34 for that game.

But that's not the full story. If you add the 5 points he got for making the free throws, and the value of the 13 field goals, which seem to be 2 points each ($13 \times 2 = 26$), we realize his game's 34 total points do not add up from those numbers ($5 + 26 = 31$).

How can we determine if those field goals were worth 2 points or 3 points?

Look below the team line score at the added description:

Three-Point goals — Detroit 10–20 (Dumars 3–7)

Only by adding the 3 baskets Dumars made from his 7 attempts shooting beyond the three-point line will his personal game total add up to 34.

The trick is to multiply those 3 baskets times 3 (3 x 3 = 9).

Subtract the number of three-pointers made (3) from the total number of field goals made (13). That becomes 13 - 3 = 10, which shows the regular two-point field goals he shot to be 10.

Multiply that number twice: 10 x 2 = 20.

Add the three-pointers he scored: 3 x 3 = 9.

Add the single points for each free throw made: 5

20 + 9 + 5 = 34.

did you know?

. . . what is meant by a triple-double?

That's the term describing the statistics of a player who achieves double numbers for three of the following five categories in the same game: points, rebounds, assists, steals, blocked shots. The term became popular in the 1980s when Magic Johnson achieved many triple-doubles for the Lakers.

Other individual efforts are noted in the bottom section. We learn that one player was disqualified for getting 6 personal fouls *(Fouled out — West)*; that the most rebounds grabbed for the Spurs *(Rodman 21)* helped San Antonio's total of 56; that Detroit's Hill was credited with 11 assists of his team's 21; that both Rodman and Miller were given technical fouls, with Miller also being ejected. We even find that the attendance of 20,443 was just under the capacity seating of 20,662.

NBA standings

EASTERN CONFERENCE

	W	L	Pct	GB	L10	Streak	Home	Away	Conf
Atlantic Division									
Orlando	41	13	.759	—	6-4	Won 1	26-1	15-12	30-9
New York	34	18	.654	6	6-4	Won 1	19-7	15-11	20-12
Boston	22	31	.415	18½	6-4	Lost 1	13-14	9-17	13-18
New Jersey	22	33	.400	19½	6-4	Won 1	15-12	7-21	13-20
Miami	20	32	.385	20	6-4	Won 2	14-12	6-20	16-20
Philadelphia	15	39	.278	26	2-8	Lost 3	8-18	7-21	8-26
Washington	12	40	.231	28	1-9	Lost 6	6-19	6-21	8-24
Central Division									
Charlotte	34	20	.630	—	6-4	Lost 1	21-7	13-13	25-12
Cleveland	32	20	.615	1	6-4	Won 1	16-10	16-10	24-11
Indiana	32	20	.615	1	7-3	Won 5	19-5	13-15	23-13
Atlanta	26	28	.481	8	6-4	Won 2	14-14	12-14	18-19
Chicago	26	28	.481	8	4-6	Lost 1	15-11	11-17	15-14
Milwaukee	21	33	.386	13	4-6	Lost 1	12-14	9-19	16-21
Detroit	19	34	.358	14½	3-7	Lost 2	15-12	4-22	13-23

WESTERN CONFERENCE

	W	L	Pct	GB	L10	Streak	Home	Away	Conf
Midwest Division									
Utah	38	16	.704	—	4-6	Lost 1	22-7	16-9	18-15
San Antonio	35	16	.686	1½	8-2	Won 4	19-6	16-10	23-11
Houston	33	19	.635	4	6-4	Won 1	17-8	16-11	17-13
Denver	23	30	.434	14½	4-6	Lost 1	15-12	8-18	14-19
Dallas	20	31	.392	16½	4-6	Lost 2	11-17	9-14	13-20
Minnesota	13	40	.245	24½	3-7	Lost 2	7-19	6-21	7-22
Pacific Division									
Phoenix	41	13	.759	—	6-4	Won 1	23-5	18-8	26-8
Seattle	37	15	.712	3	6-4	Won 2	22-5	15-10	22-12
L.A. Lakers	34	17	.667	5½	8-2	Won 4	18-6	16-11	21-10
Portland	29	23	.558	11	7-3	Won 3	18-9	11-14	19-17
Sacramento	28	23	.549	11½	4-6	Lost 3	20-7	8-16	16-14
Golden State	16	35	.314	23½	4-6	Lost 1	10-15	6-20	11-20
L.A. Clippers	9	45	.167	32	2-8	Lost 4	6-19	3-26	3-29

Team Statistics

Continue back to the middle line of the Pistons/Spurs box score.
The total points scored for each quarter are listed:

Detroit	*28*	*25*	*28*	*16 — 97*
San Antonio	*27*	*27*	*32*	*28 — 114*

You can see that although the Pistons led in the first quarter and remained close until the end of the third, they couldn't hold back the home team from putting on a winning performance in the final quarter.

The results of the Spurs' 114–97 win over the Pistons show up in the NBA standings (see page 116).

In the Western Conference, Midwest Division, San Antonio sits in second place behind Utah.

The Spurs have won *(W)* 35 games, lost *(L)* 16, giving them a .686 percentage *(Pct)* of wins–losses. They are currently 1 1/2 games behind *(GB)* the leader.

In the *(L10)* last 10 games played, the Spurs have an 8–2 record of 8 wins and 2 losses.

Their current momentum or *(Streak)* shows that they have won their last 4 games.

Playing at *(Home)*, they have 19 wins and 6 losses; on the road *(Away)*, the Spurs show 16 wins and 10 losses.

Playing against other teams in their own conference *(Conf)*, they have 23 wins and 11 losses.

Basketball's Basic Arithmetic

Here's an easy way to compile those statistics:

Win/Loss and Games-Behind-Leader:

A Team's Win/Loss Percentage $= \dfrac{\text{total wins}}{\text{total wins} + \text{losses}}$

Games-Behind-Leader $=$

$$\dfrac{\left(\begin{array}{c}\text{top team's wins minus}\\ \text{Team X's wins}\end{array}\right) + \left(\begin{array}{c}\text{Team X's losses minus}\\ \text{top team's losses}\end{array}\right)}{2}$$

Use a calculator to check how San Antonio's percentage is derived. First add their total wins plus losses (35 + 16 = 51), then divide it into the number of total wins (35).

$$\frac{35}{51} = .686$$

To find out why the Spurs are 1 1/2 games behind leader Utah Jazz, follow the formula:

$$\frac{(\ 38 - 35\ ) + (\ 16 - 16\ )}{2}$$

which becomes $\quad \dfrac{3 + 0}{2} \quad = 1.5$ (or 1 1/2)

Shooting Percentages:

Whether it's for free throws, field goals or three-pointers, here's the way to calculate a scoring percentage for either a team or individual player:

$$\text{Scoring Percentage} = \dfrac{\text{shots made}}{\text{shots attempted}}$$

To try it out, look near the back pages at the All-Time NBA Leaders for Highest Field Goal Percentage to verify Artis Gilmore's standing:

$$\frac{5,732}{9,570} = .599$$

That .599 career average continues to lead the league since Artis Gilmore retired in 1988 after 12 seasons in the NBA.

· · · · · · · · · · · · · · · · ·

did you Know?

...It's a Game For All Ages!

- Who was the youngest person to play in the NBA? Bill Willoughby was 18 years 5 months old when he played for the Atlanta Hawks. In that 1975–76 season, he came off the bench in 62 games and scored 292 points.
- Who was the oldest person to play in the NBA? Nat Hickey was 46 years old when he played one game for the Providence Steamrollers in the 1947-48 season.
- Who was the youngest coach in the NBA? Dave DeBusschere was 24 years old when he was player/coach for the Detroit Pistons in 1964–65. He held that dual role near to the end of the 1966–67 season.

...And For All Sizes

Although the average size of today's NBA player is 6-7, here are the two "bookends":

- The smallest NBA player is Muggsy Bogues (Charlotte Hornets) at 5-3 and 140 lbs.
- The tallest is Gheorghe Muresan (Washington Bullets) at 7-7 and 315 lbs.

· · · · · · · · · · · · · · · · ·

THE BAJKETBALL HALL OF FAME

11

Museums are typically quiet places with untouchable artifacts displayed in glass cases. But that's not the case at the Naismith Memorial Basketball Hall of Fame. Someone leaving the bright, roomy building is more likely to feel a bit of sweat. That follows a chance to measure your own jumping ability against the greats in the Wilson Imagymnation exhibit, or after shooting some baskets in the Spalding Shoot-Out gallery. It's a perfect way to top off an easygoing, self-guided tour through the three-level building, which is the foremost Basketball Hall of Fame in the world.

Dedicated to the memory of the game's inventor and the legacy of the sport he created, the Hall of Fame opened first in 1968 on the Springfield College campus in Massachusetts. With the roots of the game clearly set in Springfield and an increasing number of tourists coming to the "shrine of hoops," a larger, permanent building was constructed.

Ever since the new structure was completed in 1985, it has attracted about 175,000 visitors annually.

And what people discover there brings them back again. It is a chance to follow the growth of the game, from checking out a replica of the balcony where the first peach basket was hung, right through to the basketball that traveled millions of miles around Earth in 1989 aboard the space shuttle *Discovery.*

The Hall of Fame stirs up fond memories. The collection of memorabilia covers all segments of the game — men's, women's, professional, collegiate, high school, amateur, international, Olympic, referees, trainers and wheelchair.

Dr. James Naismith made many trips to foreign lands, including Japan where he gave a clinic.

Angelo (Hank) Luisetti, Stanford University 1938, famous for the one-handed set shot.

Among the trophies, medals, inscriptions and awards is the NBA Hall of Fame trophy. It is presented at the annual exhibition game in Springfield between two NBA teams to benefit the work of the Hall of Fame.

Each year in the middle of May, an induction ceremony brings dozens of Hall of Famers back to Springfield for a weekend of celebration. They welcome the newest additions to the Honors Court, the top-floor display dedicated to those who gave so much to the sport.

Members are elected in one of four categories: players, coaches, referees or contributors who helped establish the game. Nominations are presented to a Screening Committee and approved by the Honors Committee. To be considered, players and referees must be retired five years, and coaches must have coached for a minimum 25 years or have been retired five years. Contributors need to have retired.

Hall of Fame Players List

Here is a complete list of players (including pioneers, women's, college and international stars) inducted into the Naismith Memorial Basketball Hall of Fame, as of June 1995.

Kareem Abdul-
    Jabbar
Nate Archibald
Paul Arizin
Thomas Barlow
Rick Barry
Elgin Baylor
John Beckman
Walt Bellamy
Sergei Belov
Dave Bing
Carol Blazejowski
Bernard Borgmann
Bill Bradley
Joe Brennan
Al Cervi
Wilt Chamberlain
Charles "Tarzan"
    Cooper
Bob Cousy
Dave Cowens

Billy Cunningham
Bob Davies
Forrest DeBernardi
Dave DeBusschere
Henry "Dutch"
    Dehnert
Anne Donovan
Paul Endacott
Julius "Dr. J" Erving
Harold Foster
Walt Frazier
Max Friedman
Joe Fulks
Lauren "Laddie"
    Gale
Harry Gallatin
William "Pop"
    Gates
Tom Gola
Hal Greer
Robert Gruenig

Cliff Hagan
Victor Hanson
John Havlicek
Connie Hawkins
Elvin Hayes
Tommy Heinsohn
Nat Holman
Bob Houbregs
Chuck Hyatt
Dan Issel
Harry "Buddy"
    Jeannette
William "Skinny"
    Johnson
Neil Johnston
K.C. Jones
Sam Jones
Ed Krause
Bob Kurland
Bob Lanier
Joe Lapchick

Clyde Lovellette
Jerry Lucas
Angelo "Hank" Luisetti
Ed Macauley
Pete Maravich
Slater Martin
Branch McCracken
Jack McCracken
Bobby McDermott
Dick McGuire
Ann Meyers
George Mikan
Vern Mikkelsen
Cheryl Miller
Earl Monroe

Calvin Murphy
Charles Murphy
Harlan Page
Bob Pettit
Andy Phillip
James Pollard
Frank Ramsey
Willis Reed
Oscar Robertson
John Roosma
Bill Russell
John Russell
Dolph Schayes
Ernest Schmidt
John Schommer
Barney Sedran

Uljana Semjonova
Bill Sharman
Christian Steinmetz
Lusia Harris Stewart
John Thompson
Nate Thurmond
Jack Twyman
Wes Unseld
Robert Vandivier
Ed Wachter
Bill Walton
Robert Wanzer
Jerry West
Nera White
Lenny Wilkens
John Wooden

In addition to those individuals, four teams have been enshrined:

Dr. Naismith's First Team
Original Celtics
Buffalo Germans
New York Renaissance Five "The Rens"

THE RENS
Left to right:
Clarence "Fat" Jenkins, Bill Yancey, John Holt, James "Pappy" Ricks, Eyre Saitch, Charles "Tarzan" Cooper and "Wee Willie" Smith. Inset: Owner Robert L. Douglas, who organized the club in 1922-23.

The Court Speaks

12

AIRBALL - A scoring attempt in which the ball completely misses the basket and backboard.

ALLEY OOP - While jumping in midair, a player catches a pass and dunks it in to score.

ANTICIPATION - Having good "court sense," an ability to quickly reason ahead what the next shot, action or player's move is likely to be.

ASSIST - A pass from a teammate that immediately leads to a field goal.

BACKCOURT - The half-court area from the center line to the baseline which a team defends.

BACKCOURT PLAYERS - A team's two guards.

BACK DOOR - After a player passes to a teammate in the high post and draws the defenders to him, an unguarded teammate on the wing comes down the open side (back door) to receive a pass and shoot.

BALL CONTROL - Skillful dribbling, handling and passing until a player is in the best position to shoot.

BANK SHOT - A ball aimed off the backboard to go into the basket.

BASELINE - The boundary line at each end of the court.

BASELINE DRIVE - An offensive player dribbles along the defender's baseline and comes up the side of the basket to shoot.

BASKET - The net and rim; also, a score or goal.

BEHIND THE BACK - Sometimes done without looking; a tricky pass made from behind the back to a teammate.

BENCH - Substitute players; a player who has been taken out of the game and is no longer in the game is "on the bench."

BIG MAN - Usually the man who plays the center position.

BLOCK - A defensive move that diverts a shot; illegal contact that interferes with an opponent's movement.

BOMB - A shot made from a long distance.

BONUS SHOT - An additional free throw, awarded in certain penalty situations, such as after a team has committed five personal fouls in a quarter.

BOUNCE PASS - A ball passed between teammates that is bounced to get by a defender.

BOX OUT - Using your body to block an opponent by getting between him and the basket for a rebound.

BREAKAWAY - A run by an unguarded player downcourt to receive a pass with no defenders in the way.

BREAK THE ICE - A tie-breaking goal; a shot that goes in after a long, scoreless time; the first basket of a game.

BUCKET - The basket; also a goal scored: "he got four buckets."

BURN - An authoritative basket (i.e., dunk or three-pointer) that burns the opponents' momentum; also, falling along the floorboards gets a "floor burn."

BURY - A shot that goes right in the basket, often from a jump shot or three-pointer; to annihilate the opponent.

CENTER - Usually the team's tallest player, who begins the game by taking the opening tip-off, then positions himself around either basket for passes and rebounds.

CHARGING - A player control foul occurring when an offensive player runs into a stationary opponent.

CHERRY PICKING - Grabbing a rebound above the rim; hanging back at the far end of the court in order to be in position to score an easy basket.

CHUCKER - A player who shoots often.

CHUMP - An easy, can't-miss-it shot, usually a layup.

COAST TO COAST - A player races from his backcourt baseline on a fast break to the opponent's basket for a goal; or a quick play that moves from one basket, then down to the other end and maybe back to where it began.

COLD - When a shooter can't score, no matter how many attempts.

CONVERSION - A foul shot attempt that rebounds and is recovered by the offense for a quick field goal.

CRASH THE BOARDS - To rebound aggressively.

CUT - A fast offensive move without the ball to get in position for a pass.

CUTTER - An offensive player who breaks free of his guard to receive a pass.

DEAD BALL - When play stops due to a whistle, a timeout called, a foul called or a field goal made.

DEATH VALLEY - A place on the floor distant from the basket, where a player shoots from although he has little chance to score.

DENY THE BALL - A stance or move to prevent an opponent from getting possession by moving between him and the ball.

DIPSY-DOO - Fancy ball handling, either dribbling or shooting.

DISHING IT OFF - Passing the ball.

DISQUALIFICATION - To leave the game on the sixth personal foul.

DOUBLE DRIBBLE - A violation: when a player dribbles, stops, holds the ball, then dribbles again.

DOUBLE FIGURES - Statistical term to describe getting more than nine digits in a category; i.e., getting 10 or more rebounds, points or assists.

DOUBLE PUMP - Twice making a motion to shoot, which may then lead to a shot being taken.

DOUBLE TEAM - Two defensive players closely guard one offensive player.

DOUBLE VIOLATION - A violation committed by each team at the same time.

DOWN THE LANE - Advancing with the ball from the free-throw line through the painted area in front of the basket.

DOWNTOWN - An area beyond the three-point arc; a shot from "out there" is said to come from downtown.

DRAW THE FOUL - A move that causes an illegal action from an opponent.

DRIBBLE - Legal movement of the ball through controlled bounces.

DRIVE - A fast offensive move with the ball toward the basket.

DUNK (or SPIKE, JAM) - A shot made while holding the ball with one or both hands and jumping high enough to push it down into the basket.

EJECTION - Immediate dismissal from a game, usually due to a flagrant or fighting foul.

END LINE - The baseline boundary at each end of the court behind the basket.

ENGLISH - The extra bit of spin that is put on a shot.

FACE JOB - Aggressively playing defense; covering an opponent very closely.

FADEAWAY JUMPER - A jump shot taken while the player's body is moving back from the basket.

FAKE - A move that gets an opponent off balance, going in the opposite direction of your intended move.

FAST BREAK - The defense get possession under their own basket and rapidly race with the ball to the other basket in a scoring attempt before their opponents can set up a defense.

FIELD GOAL - A basket that is not a free throw; depending upon distance, can be worth two or three points.

FIGURE 8 - An offensive team moves in a figure-eight pattern with its passing and running.

FLAGRANT FOUL - Unnecessary and/or excessive contact committed against an opponent.

FLASHING - Quick movement of an offensive player from side to side through the foul lane.

FORWARD - One of two players who cover the corner areas and around the basket.

FOUL - Illegal contact between opposing players; may result in one or two foul shots.

FOUL OUT - A player who commits his sixth personal foul is disqualified from playing the rest of the game.

FOUL SHOT (or FREE THROW) - A shot to be taken from behind the free-throw line, awarded to a player who has been fouled.

FOUL TROUBLE - A player who is close to his game limit of personal fouls.

FREE-THROW LANE - The painted, 16-foot-wide area in front of the basket.

FREEZE - Controlling the ball without attempting to score.

FRONTCOURT - The half-court where a team is on the offensive and closest to the basket they need to score on.

FULL-COURT PRESS - As soon as the offense gets the ball in their backcourt, often due to a rebound, the defensive team aggressively goes after them for a sudden turnover, rather than waiting to set up at the other end of the court.

GET INSIDE - A player who positions himself between an opponent and the basket.

GIVE-AND-GO - A player passes to a teammate, then breaks in toward the basket to receive a return pass for a shot.

GLASS CLEANER - An ace rebounder, who can swipe the ball off the backboard.

GOALTENDING - A violation: interfering with the ball while it is on a downward arc to the basket. If touched by a defender, shooting team is awarded the goal; penalty for offensive goaltending is no goal and a throw-in by defense.

GUARD - Player who brings ball upcourt to direct the play; a defender who plays close to an offensive player to force a turnover.

GUNNER - A player who takes many shots from the outside, often on the run.

HACK - Chopping motion with the arm to get the ball; personal foul is called if contact is made with the player.

HALF-COURT - Area between center line and a baseline; a play in which a team spreads apart in their offensive end and passes the ball around to kill time.

HAND-CHECKING - A violation: touching a player who is being guarded so as to impede his progress.

HANG TIME - Ability to stay in the air as long as possible while attempting a shot.

HATCHET MAN - A very aggressive defensive player, who is not afraid to get physical under the basket.

HELD BALL - Two players from opposing teams grab hold of the ball simultaneously, resulting in a stoppage of play and a jump ball.

HIGH POST - The area around the free-throw circle.

HOME-COURT ADVANTAGE - The belief that a team playing in the familiar surroundings of their home court in front of their fans gives them the edge for a better performance.

HOOK SHOT - A one-handed, high-arcing shot that is difficult to block.

HOOP - Rim or basket; the act of shooting.

HOT HAND - A player who seems to have the right touch and scores a lot.

ILLEGAL DEFENSE - In the NBA, one of many defensive arrangements that do not have a defender guarding another player; essentially, if the defense is not playing man-to-man but instead is guarding an area of the floor, it's illegal.

IN THE PAINT - The free-throw lane, a painted area in front of the basket that is the prime rebound and shooting area.

INTENTIONAL FOUL - A foul committed deliberately, usually to stop the clock or as part of a plan to recover the rebound off the foul shot.

ISOLATION - A violation in which 3 or more offensive players are above the tip of the circle on the weak side, thus isolating the remaining offensive players against their defenders.

JAB - A sudden step to fake a move in one direction.

JUMP BALL - A ball tossed by an official between two opposing players, who then attempt to hit it to their teammates.

JUMP SHOT - A shot released when the player has jumped up.

KEY - The area that includes the free-throw lane and its free-throw circle, which resembles a "key."

KILL THE CLOCK - Offense controls the ball for as much of the 24-second clock or game clock as possible before releasing a shot.

LAYUP - A shot made after driving in toward the basket with a jump up to release the ball so it bounces in, usually off the backboard.

LIVE LEGS - Having great running and jumping ability.

LOOSE BALL FOUL - A foul committed when neither team has possession; the throw-in goes to the team that did not foul.

LOW POST - The area under or near the basket where the offensive center or forwards try to position themselves.

MISMATCH - A lineup between teams or players where one side has a big height advantage.

NET - The 15- to 18-inch-long hammock cord that hangs from the basket.

NOTHING BUT NET - When a shot passes through the basket without touching the rim.

OFFENSIVE FOUL - Foul committed by a team when it has possession.

ON THE LUMBER - Diving onto the floor for a loose ball.

ONE-ON-ONE - One offensive player tries to move by one defender.

ONE-HANDER - Shooting the ball with one hand.

OPEN MAN - An unguarded offensive player.

OUTLET PASS - A player grabs a rebound or steal and passes it quickly to midcourt, where the outlet man — an unguarded player — is waiting to start a fast break.

OVER THE LIMIT - When a team commits more than four fouls per quarter (or two in overtime); when a player commits his sixth personal foul of the game.

OVERPLAYING - Defensive movement or footwork that concentrates more to one side of an opponent.

OVERTIME - If the score is tied after four quarters, the game goes into a five-minute overtime period; since no game can end in a tie, five-minute overtime periods continue until there is a winner.

PALMING THE BALL - A violation: the hand is moved under the ball to scoop it up and over as dribbling continues.

PARQUET - The court's wooden playing surface, when in a checkerboard pattern.

PENALTY SITUATION - When a team has committed more than four fouls in a quarter and the opponents are awarded free throws on all subsequent fouls.

PENETRATION - An aggressive player maneuvers through a strong defense for a gutsy scoring move.

PERSONAL FOUL - An illegal action involving contact with an opponent.

PICK (or SCREEN) - An offensive strategy in which a stationary player is between the defender and his teammate, who tries to shoot or break free for a drive.

PICK AND ROLL - After setting a pick (screen) for a teammate, the player then rolls (spins) in a pivot around the defender toward the basket for a pass.

PICK-UP - A defensive player moves to guard his assigned opponent; the increasing pace of a game; a casual game played among friends ("pick-up").

PINCH POST PLAY - After passing to a teammate in the high post position, the passer speeds closely by that teammate and loses his defender, breaking open for a pass during his move to the basket.

PINE BROTHERS - The substitute players sitting on the bench, some of whom DNP (did not play) due to CD (coach's decision).

PIVOT - Keeping one foot on the floor as the other foot spins in any direction; also, the post or center position.

PLAYMAKER - The point guard.

POSITIONS - The roles given to each player; so that the team strategy can be illustrated, numbers are given accordingly: 1–point guard, 2–shooting guard, 3–small forward, 4–power forward, 5–center.

POST - A spot near the side of the free-throw lane where an offensive player will position himself; also, a player who uses his back to screen an opponent in preparing for a pass, then spins around him to score.

POST UP - A player positions himself near the free-throw lane for a pass, his back to the basket, with a defender behind him.

PRESS - Very close guarding by the defense as they try to force a turnover.

PUMP FAKE - A player pretends to go through the motion of shooting (pump) but doesn't release the ball (fake); this move either draws the defender in to make contact, drawing a foul, or allows for a clear shot as the defender's timing for an attempted block is thrown off.

RAINBOW (or RAINMAKER) - A high, looping shot.

RATTLER - A ball that rolls around the rim; if it doesn't drop in to score, it "rattles" off back into play.

REBOUND - Moving for the ball after a missed field goal or free throw when the ball bounces off the rim or backboard; a missed shot that is retrieved.

SAG - A defensive player who drops back to double-team the post.

SCOOP (or SHOVEL) - An underhand pass or shot.

SCREEN - (same as PICK)

SET SHOT - A player stands with both feet on the floor and shoots with either one or both hands.

SIXTH MAN - A substitute player; the first man in off the bench.

SHAKE AND BAKE - The fancy-stepping showmanship that might accompany a difficult shot.

SHOOT HOOPS - Casual get-together to practice shooting, often a pickup shootaround in a playground.

SHOT CLOCK - The clock that counts from 24 seconds down to zero, showing the amount of time left for the team in possession of the ball to take a shot on the basket.

SKY-HOOK - A one-handed shot released in a high arc above the head.

SKYWALK - The ability to stay airborne as if walking on air.

SLAM DUNK - A power dunk delivered with aggressive authority.

SLEEPER - Any play against an inattentive opponent.

SLOWDOWN - Any legal action, such as lengthy ball control, that eats up time on the clock to slow down the pace of the game.

SNOWBIRD - An uncontested layup.

STALL - (same as SLOWDOWN, KILL THE CLOCK)

STEAL - A move that takes the ball from an opponent without fouling.

STREAK SHOOTER - A player who goes on a shooting spree with great results, then sometimes can't score, no matter how easy the shot.

STRONG SIDE - The side of the court where the ball is being played; the area where the best players are active.

STUFF - Great skill; a dunk, with the ball placed directly in the basket.

SWING MAN - A versatile player who can play more than one position, often the shooting guard–small forward.

SWISH - A shot so accurate that the ball goes through the basket without hitting the rim, causing only a "swish" sound from the netting.

SWITCH - A move when two defenders quickly change places to guard the other's man.

TAKE THE ROOKIE TO SCHOOL - When a veteran clearly outplays a rookie, especially in one-on-one situations.

TECHNICAL FOUL - A noncontact infraction, which could be committed by a player, coach or team.

TELEGRAPH - Indicating what the next move is going to be through some inadvertent gesture.

THREE-POINT SHOT - A shot from beyond the semicircle that arcs 22 feet from the basket.

THREE-SECOND VIOLATION - An offensive player cannot stand in the free-throw lane for more than three seconds, unless he is shooting by the third second.

THREE-SIXTY - To elude a defender by spinning around in a complete circle, making a 360-degree turn.

THROW-IN - Once handed the ball by an official on the sidelines, a player has five seconds to put it into play; occurs after either a goal, some violations or once the ball has gone out of bounds.

TIP-IN - A gently touched rebound that scores.

TIP-OFF - Making contact with the ball after the referee tosses it up in the jump ball circle.

TOP OF THE KEY - The top of the jump ball circle at the end of the free-throw lane.

TOSS A BRICK - A wild shot that misses the basket and slams off the backboard.

TRAILER - An offensive player bringing up the rear on a fast break who may get into position for a better shooting opportunity on a pass from the lead player.

TRANSITION - The moment, usually after a rebound, when the defensive team goes on the offense and the offensive team shifts into defensive mode.

TRAVEL (or WALKING) - A violation: stepping with the ball without dribbling, or illegal dribbling.

TRIPLE DOUBLE - A player gets double-digit statistics in three of five categories in the same game: points, rebounds, assists, steals and blocked shots.

TRIPLE TEAM - Three defenders guard one player.

TURNAROUND JUMPER - Ball handler has his back to the basket, jumps while revolving in the air and releases a shot.

TURNOVER - Loss of possession through a steal or violation.

WEAK SIDE - The side of the court away from the action; the area with few defenders.

WEAVE - A passing/running maneuver that follows a precise pattern.

ZONE DEFENSE - Each defense player covers a court area instead of an offensive player (illegal in the NBA).

NBA Team Directory

ATLANTA HAWKS
One CNN Center, Suite 405
South Tower
Atlanta, Georgia 30303
(404) 827-3800

Team origin: Tri-City Blackhawks (1949–51); Milwaukee Hawks (1951–55); St. Louis Hawks (1955–68); Atlanta Hawks since 1968

Home court: The Omni, built in 1972, seats 16,365

Team colors: red, yellow, gold and black

BOSTON CELTICS
151 Merrimac Street
Boston, Massachusetts 02114
(617) 523-6050

Team origin: original NBA member since 1946

Home court: FleetCenter, built in 1995, seats 18,400

Team colors: green, white and black

CHARLOTTE HORNETS
100 Hive Drive
Charlotte, North Carolina 28217
(704) 357-0252

Team origin: Charlotte Hornets since 1988
Home court: Charlotte Coliseum, built in 1988, seats 23,698
Team colors: teal, purple, warm red and white

CHICAGO BULLS
1901 West Madison
Chicago, Illinois 60612
(312) 455-4000

Team origin: Chicago Bulls since 1966
Home court: United Center, built in 1994, seats 21,500
Team colors: red, white and black

CLEVELAND CAVALIERS
One Center Court
Cleveland, Ohio 44115
(216) 420-2000

Team origin: Cleveland Cavaliers since 1971
Home court: Gund Arena, built in 1994, seats 20,562
Team colors: blue, orange and black

DALLAS MAVERICKS

777 Sports Street
Dallas, Texas 75207
(214) 748-1808

Team origin: Dallas Mavericks since 1980
Home court: Reunion Arena, built in 1980, seats 17,502
Team colors: blue and green

DENVER NUGGETS

1635 Clay Street
P.O. Box 4658
Denver, Colorado 80204
(303) 893-6700

Team origin: Denver Rockets (ABA) 1967–76; Denver Nuggets (NBA) since 1976
Home court: McNichols Sports Arena, built in 1975, seats 17,171
Team colors: gold, red and blue

DETROIT PISTONS

Two Championship Drive
Auburn Hills, Michigan 48326
(810) 377-0100

Team origin: Fort Wayne Pistons, 1948–57; Detroit Pistons since 1957
Home court: The Palace of Auburn Hills, built in 1988, seats 21,454
Team colors: red, white and blue

GOLDEN STATE WARRIORS
7000 Coliseum Way
Oakland, California 94621
(510) 638-6300

Team origin: original NBA member as Philadelphia Warriors, 1946–62; San Francisco Warriors 1962–71; Golden State Warriors since 1971
Home court: Oakland Coliseum Arena, built in 1966, seats 15,025
Team colors: gold and blue

HOUSTON ROCKETS
Ten Greenway Plaza East
Houston, Texas 77046
(713) 627-3865

Team origin: San Diego Rockets, 1967–71; Houston Rockets, since 1971
Home court: The Summit, built in 1975, seats 16,311
Team colors: blue, metallic blue, red and silver

INDIANA PACERS
300 East Market Street
Indianapolis, Indiana 46204
(317) 263-2100

Team origin: Indiana Pacers (ABA) 1967–76; Indiana Pacers (NBA) since 1976
Home court: Market Square Arena, built in 1974, seats 16,530
Team colors: blue and yellow

LOS ANGELES CLIPPERS
3939 South Figueroa Street
Los Angeles, California 90037
(213) 745-0400

Team origin: Buffalo Braves, 1970–78; San Diego Clippers, 1978–84; Los Angeles Clippers since 1984
Home court: Los Angeles Memorial Sports Arena, built in 1959, seats 16,005
Team colors: red, white and blue

LOS ANGELES LAKERS
3900 West Manchester Street
P.O. Box 10
Los Angeles, California 90305
(310) 419-3100

Team origin: Minneapolis Lakers, 1948–60; Los Angeles Lakers since 1960
Home court: The Great Western Forum, built in 1967, seats 17,505
Team colors: royal purple and gold

MIAMI HEAT
701 Arena Boulevard
Miami, Florida 33136
(305) 577-4328

Team origin: Miami Heat since 1988
Home court: Miami Arena, built in 1988, seats 15,200
Team colors: red, yellow, black and white

MILWAUKEE BUCKS
1001 North Fourth Street
Milwaukee, Wisconsin 53203
(414) 227-0500

Team origin: Milwaukee Bucks since 1968
Home court: Bradley Center, built in 1988, seats 18,633
Team colors: forest green, purple and silver

MINNESOTA TIMBERWOLVES
600 First Avenue North
Minneapolis, Minnesota 55403
(612) 673-1600

Team origin: Minnesota Timberwolves since 1989
Home court: Target Center, built in 1990, seats 19,006
Team colors: royal blue, kelly green and silver

NEW JERSEY NETS
405 Murray Hill Parkway
East Rutherford, New Jersey 07073
(201) 935-8888

Team origin: New Jersey Americans (ABA) 1967–68; New York
Nets (ABA) 1968–76; New York Nets (NBA) 1976; New Jersey
Nets (NBA) since 1977
Home court: Meadowlands Arena, built in 1981, seats 20,029
Team colors: red, white and blue

NEW YORK KNICKS
Two Pennsylvania Plaza
New York, New York 10121
(212) 465-6499

Team origin: original NBA member since 1946
Home court: Madison Square Garden, built in 1968, seats 19,763
Team colors: orange, blue and silver

ORLANDO MAGIC
One Magic Place
Orlando, Florida 32801
(407) 649-3200

Team origin: Orlando Magic since 1989
Home court: Orlando Arena, built in 1989, seats 16,010
Team colors: black, silver and blue

PHILADELPHIA 76ers
P.O. Box 25040
Broad Street and Pattison Avenue
Philadelphia, Pennsylvania 19147
(215) 339-7600

Team origin: Syracuse Nationals, 1949–63; Philadelphia 76ers since 1963
Home court: Core States Spectrum, built in 1967, seats 18,168
Team colors: red, white and blue

PHOENIX SUNS
Phoenix Suns Plaza
201 East Jefferson Street
Phoenix, Arizona 85004
(602) 379-7900

Team origin: Phoenix Suns since 1968
Home court: America West Arena, built in 1992, seats 19,023
Team colors: purple, orange and copper

PORTLAND TRAIL BLAZERS
One North Center Court
Portland, Oregon 97232
(503) 234-9291

Team origin: Portland Trail Blazers since 1970
Home court: Rose Garden, built in 1995, seats 21,700
Team colors: scarlet, black and white

SACRAMENTO KINGS
One Sports Parkway
Sacramento, California 95834
(916) 928-0000

Team origin: Rochester Royals, 1948–57; Cincinnati Royals, 1957–72; Kansas City-Omaha Kings, 1972–75; Kansas City Kings, 1975–85; Sacramento Kings since 1985
Home court: ARCO Arena, built in 1988, seats 17,317
Team colors: purple, black and silver

SAN ANTONIO SPURS
100 Montana Street
San Antonio, Texas 78203
(210) 554-7700

Team origin: Dallas Chaparalls (ABA), 1967–70 and 1971–73;
Texas Chaparalls, (ABA) 1970–71; San Antonio (ABA) 1973–76;
San Antonio Spurs (NBA) since 1976
Home court: Alamodome, built in 1993, seats 20,662
Team colors: metallic silver, black, teal, fuchsia and orange

SEATTLE SUPERSONICS
190 Queen Anne Avenue North,
Suite 200
Seattle, Washington 98109
(206) 281-5800

Team origin: Seattle SuperSonics since 1967
Home court: Key Arena at the Seattle Center, built in 1962
(rebuilt in 1995), seats 17,100
Team colors: yellow, green, red and bronze

TORONTO RAPTORS
20 Bay Street, Suite 1702
Toronto, Ontario M5J 2N8
(416) 214-2255

Team origin: Toronto Raptors since 1995
Home court: SkyDome, built in 1989, seats 23,000
Team colors: purple, red, black, silver

UTAH JAZZ
301 West So. Temple
Salt Lake City, Utah 84101
(801) 325-2500

Team origin: New Orleans Jazz, 1974–79; Utah Jazz since 1979
Home court: Delta Center, built in 1991, seats 19,911
Team colors: purple, green and gold

VANCOUVER GRIZZLIES
788 Beatty Street, Third Floor, #201
Vancouver, British Columbia
V6B 2M1
(604) 688-5867
Team origin: Vancouver Grizzlies since 1995
Home court: General Motors Place, built in 1995, seats 20,004
Team colors: green, brown, black, red

WASHINGTON BULLETS
One Harry S. Truman Drive
Landover, Maryland 20785
(301) 773-2255

Team origin: Chicago Packers, 1961–62; Chicago Zephyrs, 1962–63; Baltimore Bullets, 1963–73; Capital Bullets, 1973–74; Washington Bullets since 1974
Home court: USAir Arena, built in 1973, seats 18,756
Team colors: red, white and blue

Superstar Statistics

14

All-Time NBA MVPs
Maurice Podoloff Trophy

1956	Bob Pettit, St. Louis		1976	Kareem Abdul-Jabbar, LA Lakers
1957	Bob Cousy, Boston		1977	Kareem Abdul-Jabbar, LA Lakers
1958	Bill Russell, Boston		1978	Bill Walton, Portland
1959	Bob Pettit, St. Louis		1979	Moses Malone, Houston
1960	Wilt Chamberlain, Philadelphia		1980	Kareem Abdul-Jabbar, LA Lakers
1961	Bill Russell, Boston		1981	Julius Erving, Philadelphia
1962	Bill Russell ,Boston		1982	Moses Malone, Houston
1963	Bill Russell, Boston		1983	Moses Malone, Philadelphia
1964	Oscar Robertson, Cincinnati		1984	Larry Bird, Boston
1965	Bill Russell, Boston		1985	Larry Bird, Boston
1966	Wilt Chamberlain, Philadelphia		1986	Larry Bird, Boston
1967	Wilt Chamberlain, Philadelphia		1987	Magic Johnson, LA Lakers
1968	Wilt Chamberlain, Philadelphia		1988	Michael Jordan, Chicago
1969	Wes Unseld, Baltimore		1989	Magic Johnson, LA Lakers
1970	Willis Reed, New York		1990	Magic Johnson, LA Lakers
1971	Kareem Abdul-Jabbar, Milwaukee		1991	Michael Jordan, Chicago
1972	Kareem Abdul-Jabbar, Milwaukee		1992	Michael Jordan, Chicago
1973	Dave Cowens, Boston		1993	Charles Barkley, Phoenix
1974	Kareem Abdul-Jabbar, Milwaukee		1994	Hakeem Olajuwon, Houston
1975	Bob McAdoo, Buffalo		1995	David Robinson, San Antonio

NBA Champions: Year-by-Year

Year	Dates	Winner (Coach)	Loser (Coach)	Games
1947	Apr. 16-Apr. 22	Philadelphia (Gottlieb)	Chicago (Olsen)	4-1
1948	Apr. 10-Apr. 21	Baltimore (Jeannette)	Philadelphia (Gottlieb)	4-2
1949	Apr. 4-Apr. 13	Minneapolis (Kundla)	Washington (Auerbach)	4-2
1950	Apr. 8-Apr. 23	Minneapolis (Kundla)	*Syracuse (Cervi)	4-2
1951	Apr. 7-Apr. 21	Rochester (Harrison)	New York (Lapchick)	4-3
1952	Apr. 12-Apr. 25	Minneapolis (Kundla)	New York (Lapchick)	4-3
1953	Apr. 4-Apr. 10	*Minneapolis (Kundla)	New York (Lapchick)	4-1
1954	Mar. 31-Apr. 12	*Minneapolis (Kundla)	Syracuse (Cervi)	4-3
1955	Mar. 31-Apr. 10	*Syracuse (Cervi)	*Ft. Wayne (Eckman)	4-3
1956	Mar. 31-Apr. 7	*Philadelphia (Senesky)	Ft. Wayne (Eckman)	4-1
1957	Mar. 30-Apr. 13	*Boston (Auerbach)	St. Louis (Macauley)	4-3
1958	Mar. 29-Apr. 12	St. Louis (Hannum)	*Boston (Auerbach)	4-2
1959	Apr. 4-Apr. 9	*Boston (Auerbach)	Minneapolis (Kundla)	4-0
1960	Mar. 27-Apr. 9	*Boston (Auerbach)	St. Louis (Macauley)	4-3
1961	Apr. 2-Apr. 11	*Boston (Auerbach)	St. Louis (Seymour)	4-1
1962	Apr. 7-Apr. 18	*Boston (Auerbach)	LA Lakers (Schaus)	4-3
1963	Apr. 14-Apr. 24	*Boston (Auerbach)	LA Lakers (Schaus)	4-2
1964	Apr. 18-Apr. 26	*Boston (Auerbach)	San Francisco (Hannum)	4-1
1965	Apr. 18-Apr. 23	*Boston (Auerbach)	LA Lakers (Schaus)	4-1
1966	Apr. 18-Apr. 26	Boston (Auerbach)	LA Lakers (Schaus)	4-3
1967	Apr. 17-Apr. 28	*Philadelphia (Hannum)	San Francisco (Sharman)	4-2
1968	Apr. 21-May 2	Boston (Russell)	LA Lakers (van Breda Kolff)	4-2
1969	Apr. 23-May 3	Boston (Russell)	LA Lakers (van Breda Kolff)	4-3
1970	Apr. 24-May 8	*New York (Holzman)	LA Lakers (Mullaney)	4-3
1971	Apr. 21-Apr. 30	*Milwaukee (Costello)	Baltimore (Shue)	4-0
1972	Apr. 28-May 7	*LA Lakers (Sharman)	New York (Holzman)	4-1
1973	May 1-May 10	New York (Holzman)	LA Lakers (Sharman)	4-1
1974	Apr. 28-May 12	Boston (Heinsohn)	Milwaukee (Costello)	4-3
1975	May 18-May 25	Golden State (Attles)	*Washington (Jones)	4-0
1976	May 23-June 6	Boston (Heinsohn)	Phoenix (MacLeod)	4-2
1977	May 22-June 5	Portland (Ramsay)	Philadelphia (Shue)	4-2
1978	May 21-June 7	Washington (Motta)	Seattle (Wilkens)	4-3
1979	May 20-June 1	Seattle (Wilkens)	*Washington (Motta)	4-1
1980	May 4-May 16	LA Lakers (Westhead)	Philadelphia (Cunningham)	4-2
1981	May 5-May 14	*Boston (Fitch)	Houston (Harris)	4-2
1982	May 27-June 8	LA Lakers (Riley)	Philadelphia (Cunningham)	4-2
1983	May 22-May 31	*Philadelphia (Cunningham)	LA Lakers (Riley)	4-0
1984	May 27-June 12	*Boston (Jones)	LA Lakers (Riley)	4-3
1985	May 27-June 9	LA Lakers (Riley)	*Boston (Jones)	4-2
1986	May 26-June 8	*Boston (Jones)	Houston (Fitch)	4-2
1987	June 2-June 14	*LA Lakers (Riley)	Boston (Jones)	4-2
1988	June 7-June 21	*LA Lakers (Riley)	Detroit (Daly)	4-3
1989	June 6-June 13	*Detroit (Daly)	LA Lakers (Riley)	4-0
1990	June 5-June 14	*Detroit (Daly)	Portland (Adelman)	4-1
1991	June 2-June 12	Chicago (Jackson)	LA Lakers (Dunleavy)	4-1
1992	June 3-June 14	*Chicago (Jackson)	Portland (Adelman)	4-2
1993	June 9-June 20	Chicago (Jackson)	*Phoenix (Westphal)	4-2
1994	June 8-June 22	Houston (Tomjanovich)	New York (Riley)	4-3
1995	June 7-June 14	Houston (Tomjanovich)	Orlando (Hill)	4-0

*Had best record (or tied for best record) during regular season.

NBA Finals Most Valuable Player

1970	Willis Reed, New York	1983	Moses Malone, Philadelphia
1971	Kareem Abdul-Jabbar, Milwaukee	1984	Larry Bird, Boston
1972	Wilt Chamberlain, LA Lakers	1985	Kareem Abdul-Jabbar, LA Lakers
1973	Willis Reed, New York	1986	Larry Bird, Boston
1974	John Havlicek, Boston	1987	Magic Johnson, LA Lakers
1975	Rick Barry, Golden State	1988	James Worthy, LA Lakers
1976	Jo Jo White, Boston	1989	Joe Dumars, Detroit
1977	Bill Walton, Portland	1990	Isiah Thomas, Detroit
1978	Wes Unseld, Washington	1991	Michael Jordan, Chicago
1979	Dennis Johnson, Seattle	1992	Michael Jordan, Chicago
1980	Magic Johnson, LA Lakers	1993	Michael Jordan, Chicago
1981	Cedric Maxwell, Boston	1994	Hakeem Olajuwon, Houston
1982	Magic Johnson, LA Lakers	1995	Hakeem Olajuwon, Houston

All-Time NBA Leaders (includes 1994-95 season)

1994-95 active players in caps

MOST GAMES PLAYED

Player	Games
Kareem Abdul-Jabbar	1,560
ROBERT PARISH	1,494
MOSES MALONE	1,329
Elvin Hayes	1,303
John Havlicek	1,270
Paul Silas	1,254
Alex English	1,193
TREE ROLLINS	1,156
JAMES EDWARDS	1,140
Hal Greer	1,122
BUCK WILLIAMS	1,122

HIGHEST FIELD GOAL PERCENTAGE
(2,000 FGM MINIMUM)

Player	FGA	FGM	Pct.
Artis Gilmore	9,570	5,732	.599
MARK WEST	3,958	2,330	.589
SHAQUILLE O'NEAL	4,489	2,616	.583
Steve Johnson	4,965	2,841	.572
Darryl Dawkins	6,079	3,477	.572
JAMES DONALDSON	5,442	3,105	.571
Jeff Ruland	3,734	2,105	.564
Kareem Abdul-Jabbar	28,307	15,837	.559
OTIS THORPE	9,515	5,283	.555
CHARLES BARKLEY	12,285	6,813	.555

HIGHEST FREE THROW PERCENTAGE
(1,200 FTM MINIMUM)

Player	FTA	FTM	Pct.
MARK PRICE	2,078	1,883	.906
Rick Barry	4,243	3,818	.900
Calvin Murphy	3,864	3,445	.892
SCOTT SKILES	1,731	1,540	.890
Larry Bird	4,471	3,960	.886
Bill Sharman	3,559	3,143	.883
REGGIE MILLER	3,624	3,186	.879
RICKY PIERCE	3,142	2,751	.876
Kiki Vandeweghe	3,997	3,484	.872
JEFF MALONE	3,351	2,918	.871

HIGHEST 3-POINT FIELD GOAL PERCENTAGE
(100 3FGM MINIMUM)

Player	3FGA	3FGM	Pct.
STEVE KERR	617	288	.467
Drazen Petrovic	583	255	.437
B.J. ARMSTRONG	650	284	.437
DANA BARROS	1,453	606	.417
MARK PRICE	1,960	802	.409
Trent Tucker	1,410	575	.408
DALE ELLIS	2,783	1,119	.402
HERSEY HAWKINS	1,705	685	.402
Craig Hodges	1,408	563	.400
KENNY SMITH	1,292	514	.398

MOST TOTAL REBOUNDS

Player	Rebounds
Wilt Chamberlain	23,924
Bill Russell	21,620
Kareem Abdul-Jabbar	17,440
Elvin Hayes	16,279
MOSES MALONE	16,212
Nate Thurmond	14,464
ROBERT PARISH	14,323
Walt Bellamy	14,241
Wes Unseld	13,769
Jerry Lucas	12,942

MOST ASSISTS

Player	Assists
JOHN STOCKTON	10,394
Magic Johnson	9,921
Oscar Robertson	9,887
Isiah Thomas	9,061
Maurice Cheeks	7,392
Len Wilkens	7,211
Bob Cousy	6,955
Guy Rodgers	6,917
Nate Archibald	6,476
John Lucas	6,454

HIGHEST SCORING AVERAGE
(400 GAMES OR 10,000 POINTS MINIMUM)

Player	G.	Pts.	Avg.
MICHAEL JORDAN	684	21,998	32.2
Wilt Chamberlain	1045	31,419	30.1
Elgin Baylor	846	23,149	27.4
Jerry West	932	25,192	27.0
Bob Pettit	792	20,880	26.4
George Gervin	791	20,708	26.2
KARL MALONE	816	21,237	26.0
DOMINIQUE WILKINS	984	25,389	25.8
DAVID ROBINSON	475	12,209	25.7
Oscar Robertson	1040	26,710	25.7

MOST POINTS

Player	Points
Kareem Abdul-Jabbar	38,387
Wilt Chamberlain	31,419
MOSES MALONE	27,409
Elvin Hayes	27,313
Oscar Robertson	26,710
John Havlicek	26,395
Alex English	25,613
DOMINIQUE WILKINS	25,389
Jerry West	25,192
Adrian Dantley	23,177

Active NBA Leaders (Career Statistics)

Players who were on active rosters or on injured list during 1994-95 season

MOST GAMES PLAYED

Player	Games
Robert Parish	1,494
Moses Malone	1,329
Tree Rollins	1,156
James Edwards	1,140
Buck Williams	1,122
Tom Chambers	1,094
Danny Ainge	1,042
Herb Williams	1,004
Dominique Wilkins	984
Rick Mahorn	970

HIGHEST FIELD GOAL PERCENTAGE (2,000 FGM MINIMUM)

Player	FGA	FGM	Pct.
Mark West	3,958	2,330	.589
Shaquille O'Neal	4,489	2,616	.583
James Donaldson	5,442	3,105	.571
Otis Thorpe	9,515	5,283	.555
Charles Barkley	12,285	6,813	.555
Jeff Ruland	3,734	2,105	.564
Buck Williams	9,674	5,362	.554
Kevin McHale	12,334	6,830	.554
Larry Nance	11,350	6,217	.548
Robert Parish	16,433	8,909	.542
Dennis Rodman	3,751	2,016	.537
Brad Daugherty	6,583	3,527	.536

HIGHEST FREE THROW PERCENTAGE (1,200 FTM MINIMUM)

Player	FTA	FTM	Pct.
Mark Price	2,078	1,883	.906
Scott Skiles	1,731	1,540	.890
Reggie Miller	3,624	3,186	.879
Ricky Pierce	3,459	3,033	.877
Jeff Malone	3,351	2,918	.871
Hersey Hawkins	2,887	2,502	.867
Micheal Williams	1,714	1,485	.866
Jeff Hornacek	2,132	1,840	.863
Chris Mullin	3,480	3,000	.862
Michael Adams	2,508	2,132	.850

HIGHEST 3-POINT FIELD GOAL PERCENTAGE (250 3FGM MINIMUM)

Player	3FGA	3FGM	Pct.
Steve Kerr	617	288	.467
B.J. Armstrong	650	284	.437
Dana Barros	1,453	606	.417
Mark Price	1,960	802	.409
Dale Ellis	2,783	1,119	.402
Hersey Hawkins	1,705	685	.402
Kenny Smith	1,292	514	.398
Dennis Scott	1,431	567	.396
Reggie Miller	2,622	1,035	.395
Dell Curry	1,588	623	.392

MOST REBOUNDS

Player	Rebounds
Moses Malone	16,212
Robert Parish	14,323
Buck Williams	12,033
Hakeem Olajuwon	10,239
Charles Barkley	9,490
Karl Malone	8,929
Dennis Rodman	8,489
Charles Oakley	8,130
Kevin Willis	7,952
Otis Thorpe	7,878

MOST ASSISTS

Player	Assists
John Stockton	10,394
Derek Harper	5,484
Muggsy Bogues	5,469
Terry Porter	5,319
Kevin Johnson	5,272
Mark Jackson	5,255
Sleepy Floyd	5,175
Clyde Drexler	5,087
Doc Rivers	4,766
Nate McMillan	4,501

HIGHEST SCORING AVERAGE (400 GAMES OR 10,000 POINTS MINIMUM)

Player	G.	Pts.	Avg.
Michael Jordan	684	21,998	32.2
Karl Malone	816	21,237	26.0
Dominique Wilkins	984	25,389	25.8
David Robinson	475	12,209	25.7
Hakeem Olajuwon	828	19,904	24.0
Patrick Ewing	759	18,077	23.8
Charles Barkley	819	19,091	23.3
Mitch Richmond	519	11,781	22.7
Chris Mullin	653	14,243	21.8
Clyde Drexler	902	18,789	20.8

MOST POINTS

Player	Points
Moses Malone	27,409
Dominique Wilkins	25,389
Robert Parish	22,883
Michael Jordan	21,998
Karl Malone	21,237
Tom Chambers	20,024
Hakeem Olajuwon	19,904
Charles Barkley	19,091
Clyde Drexler	18,789
Patrick Ewing	18,077

All-Time NBA Rookies of the Year
Eddie Gottlieb Trophy

Year	Player	Year	Player
1948	Paul Hoffman, Baltimore	1972	Sidney Wicks, Portland
1949	Howie Shannon, Providence	1973	Bob McAdoo, Buffalo
1950	Alex Groza, Indianapolis	1974	Ernie DiGregorio, Buffalo
1951	Paul Arizin, Philadelphia	1975	Jamaal Wilkes, Golden State
1952	(tie) Bill Tosheff, Indianapolis	1976	Alvan Adams, Phoenix
	Mel Hutchins, Milwaukee	1977	Adrian Dantley, Buffalo
1953	Don Meineke, Fort Wayne	1978	Walter Davis, Phoenix
1954	Ray Felix, Baltimore	1979	Phil Ford, Kansas City
1955	Bob Pettit, Milwaukee	1980	Larry Bird, Boston
1956	Maurice Stokes, Rochester	1981	Darrell Griffith, Utah
1957	Tom Heinsohn, Boston	1982	Buck Williams, New Jersey
1958	Woody Sauldsberry, Philadelphia	1983	Terry Cummings, San Diego
1959	Elgin Baylor, Minneapolis	1984	Ralph Sampson, Houston
1960	Wilt Chamberlain, Philadelphia	1985	Michael Jordan, Chicago
1961	Oscar Robertson, Cincinnati	1986	Patrick Ewing, New York
1962	Walt Bellamy, Chicago	1987	Chuck Person, Indiana
1963	Terry Dischinger, Chicago	1988	Mark Jackson, New York
1964	Jerry Lucas, Cincinnati	1989	Mitch Richmond, Golden State
1965	Willis Reed, New York	1990	David Robinson, San Antonio
1966	Rick Barry, San Francisco	1991	Derrick Coleman, New Jersey
1967	Dave Bing, Detroit	1992	Larry Johnson, Charlotte
1968	Earl Monroe, Baltimore	1993	Shaquille O'Neal, Orlando
1969	Wes Unseld, Baltimore	1994	Chris Webber, Golden State
1970	Kareem Abdul-Jabbar, Milwaukee	1995	(tie) Grant Hill, Detroit
1971	(tie) Dave Cowens, Boston		Jason Kidd, Dallas
	Geoff Petrie, Portland		

ACKNOWLEDGEMENTS

Special thanks to an author's Dream Team at Random House of Canada: Doug Pepper, Sarah Davies, Sharon Klein, Kathryn Mulders, Alan Terakawa and Sharon Foster.

Thanks also to Robert and Patricia Sutherland-Cohen for their assistance and inspiration; to Wayne Patterson at the Naismith Memorial Basketball Hall of Fame; and to Frank Fochetta, Diane Naughton, Alex Sachare, Mark Seigerman and Deborah Gottesfeld at the NBA.

PHOTOGRAPH AND ILLUSTRATION CREDITS

The charts illustrated on pages 108 and 112 and logos found on pages 8, 10, 76, 77, 78, 80, 137-146 are © by NBA Properties, Inc.

Court dimensions on page 21 are from *The Sporting News Official NBA Guide, 1994-1995 Edition,* © 1994 by NBA Properties, Inc.

The referee signals on pages 55-57 are from the *1994-1995 Official NBA Rules,* © 1994 by NBA Properties, Inc.

Playoff structure on page 88 is © by NBA Properties, Inc.

Photographs on the front cover and pages 65-72 are courtesy of NBA Photos:
Cover: © Nathaniel S. Butler/NBA Photos
Page 65: © Fernando Medina/NBA Photos
Page 66: © Nathaniel S. Butler/NBA Photos
Page 67: top, © Andrew D. Bernstein/NBA Photos; bottom, © Nathaniel S. Butler/NBA Photos
Page 68: top right, © Lou Capozzola/NBA Photos; top left, © Rocky Widner/ NBA Photos; bottom right, © Nathaniel S. Butler/NBA Photos; bottom left, © Andy Hayt/NBA Photos
Page 69: © Nathaniel S. Butler/NBA Photos
Page 70: © Allen Einstein/NBA Photos
Page 71: top, © Bill Baptist/NBA Photos; bottom right, © Lou Capozzola/NBA Photos; bottom left, © Gregg Forwerck/NBA Photos
Page 72: © Andy Hayt/NBA Photos

Photographs on pages 12, 22, 121 and 123 and art on page 19 from **Spalding's Official Basket Ball Guide 1908-9** (New York: American Sports Publishing Company, 1908), are courtesy of the Naismith Memorial Basketball Hall of Fame.

All additional illustrations by Glenn Mielke/Three in a Box.